The Sinking of Noah's Ark

TrysDan Roberts

"The Sinking of Noah's Ark." ISBN 1-58939-219-1 (softcover version).

Library of Congress Control Number: 2002110973.

Published 2002 by Virtualbookworm.com Publishing Inc., P.O. Box 9949, College Station, TX , 77842, US. ©2002 TrysDan Roberts. All rights reserved. No part of this publication may be reproduced, stored in a retrieval system, or transmitted in any form or by any means, electronic, mechanical, recording or otherwise, without the prior written permission of TrysDan Roberts.

Manufactured in the United States of America.

For:

*Elizabeth
Dorothy
Russell
Ishmael*

Our deepest fear is not that we are inadequate. Our deepest fear is that we are powerful beyond measure. It is our light, not our darkness, that most frightens us.

We ask ourselves, "Who am I to be brilliant, gorgeous, talented and fabulous?" Actually, who are you not to be? You are a child of God. Your playing small doesn't save the world. There's nothing enlightening about shrinking so that other people won't feel insecure around you.

We are born to make manifest the glory of God that is within us. It's not just in some of us; it's in everyone.

As we let our light shine, we unconsciously give other people permission to do the same. As we are liberated from our own fear, our presence automatically liberates others.

Nelson Mandela
Inaugural Speech. 1994

"Noah, how do I get to heaven?"

That's just great, *I fumed silently. I was about to plunge into one of my most treasured sources of knowledge, National Geographic Magazine, and enter the lost world of the tyrannosaurus rex and the pterodactyl. This insidious question interrupting my journey does not belong in this world. Here, such a place as heaven does not exist.*

Reluctantly glancing up from the page, I witness the hopeful eyes of innocence gazing into mine. After a moment of careful thought, I decide he is not ready for the truth.

"You have to hijack Santa's sleigh."

That was the first and last piece of spiritual advice I have ever given my little brother. Looking back, sixteen years later, I realize that I should have taken my responsibilities as mentor more seriously. But that was how the King men addressed such a vacant question. I was instilled with the family code of honor at a young age. The code is simple: Provide a life for your family that is better than the life your father provided. There was no room for philosophical discussions, as they didn't put food on the table.

In retrospect, that was the meaning of life as I had come to understand it.

Today, at the age of thirty, I find myself acknowledging the beginning. As I sit in this salt-blemished rowboat, conceding to this new frontier that I have lain out in front of me, I cannot help but feel like the victim of a bittersweet prank.

Gazing across the glistening water, I reflect on the sparse community responsible for my existence, and as the fog gently lifts from the barren shoreline, it is clear that I now travel the path I have struggled all of my life not only to avoid, but to even acknowledge. For the first time in my life, my future is a blank page.

But how I arrived at this path is a greater mystery. When reflecting on the event, I cannot determine whether it can be described as fiction or non-fiction, as fantasy or reality. I can only conclude that the events felt as real as the kiss of the crisp sea air on my crimsoned cheek, and its realness irrevocably shattered the foundation of my existence. The ideals and beliefs guiding my passage through time were incinerated in an instant.

In essence, life as I once interpreted it is nothing more than a myth embroidered in a web of truths and lies. In an endless struggle to restore the ruins that mournfully rest within me, I now realize that unraveling the web is the passport required for the new journey.

Chapter I

Noah King is from Walden's Cove, a tiny community resting on the most southeastern point of Maine. The town sits on a barren island lying at the tip of a peninsula that stretches out into the Atlantic Ocean, allowing the water to completely envelop the community. Except for a narrow causeway extending a length of about one hundred and fifty feet, the inhabitants are completely cut off from the mainland.

A tourist from a densely populated city may describe the town as quaint or charming, but as a boy, Noah seriously disagreed. In the early mornings of his innocent youth, as soon as the fog set in, he would imagine a huge pillow descending upon him. Looking through Noah's eyes, Walden's Cove was a prison, and time was its most prized captive.

⚜ ⚜ ⚜

Noah was not an average kid. Playing sports and hanging out with the guys was not a passion of his, as he knew that he wanted more from life than the town could give him. He longed to go to college, become an educated man, and travel to the faraway places that he spent hours reading about. He wanted to be a part of the bigger picture.

Noah was an explorer—a hopeless dreamer. He liked to think of himself as a modern-day Viking, without the horns. On many Saturday afternoons, he sat by the causeway imagining what lay on the other side, what mysterious treasures impatiently waited for his discovery.

Sometimes he would slowly walk to the other side, turn around, and stare into his present, imagining that he was in the future, peering into the past, wondering what historical events had occurred in between.

⚜ ⚜ ⚜

As a child, Noah's perception of the community and its inhabitants was that of disgruntled adolescence. The houses and people were indistinguishable. Most dwellings varied in color, but when he observed them as a whole, one color dominated—a dismal gray.

According to Noah, the people inhabiting the houses were not much different. One yearly event reflecting the essence of the community was Halloween. Noah and his little brother, Aidan, would roam up and down the neighborhood streets. Dressed in their father's faded and torn fishing shirts, completed with old stained jeans riddled with frayed holes, they were greeted at each door by cheerful faces resembling the inhabitants of the previous house. It was as if time was caught in a repetitive loop, always returning them to the previous house when the door started to open.

The delighted grins converging upon them would laugh and declare, "Well, aren't you two a couple of sweet-lookin' hobos."

Sweet hobo, Noah mused to himself. *An unusual phrase to apply to a homeless person.* Although he would have loved to point out the paradox to them, the fear of losing even one sweet morsel compelled him to hold his tongue.

ಌ ಌ ಌ

The Fishing Wharf, stationed at the foot of the cove, was the economic force keeping the town afloat. Dilapidated fishing houses dotted the rocky shoreline. Throughout Noah's childhood, approximately seventy-five fishing boats painted the Cove. There were green boats, blue boats, boats of almost any color imaginable, giving the impression of life. There were also boats of different sizes and lengths. The smallest ones, known as dories, are high-sided, flat-bottomed, sharp-bowed rowboats, used in many New England fisheries since the eighteenth century.

Noah's father's boat, the largest of the fleet, held more crew and more lobster traps. Stretching an intimidating thirty-five feet, the vessel boasted a small forward cabin and a windshield shelter for the helmsman. She also had a round bottom with a double-wedge hull. The hulls were traditionally built of wood, but fiberglass hulls began to replace them by the early 1960's. As an opponent of progress, his father made sure the hull was constructed of wood.

ಌ ಌ ಌ

One might think the fishermen played a chief role in establishing the traditions and values of the community, but that was not the case. The major social and cultural influence rested within an institution Noah refused to acknowledge—the Church. This seemingly harmless building, with its waned white exterior, rested on a steep, rocky hill towering above the community.

Noah often gazed up at that towering fortress, imagining it suspiciously glaring down upon him, forever keeping a watchful eye, a reminder to follow the rules…or suffer the consequences.

The first twelve years of the King family life resulted in the creation of Noah and Aidan. Paul King, a strong and proud man, provided the family with a comfortable living—a modest three-bedroom bungalow with all of the necessities at arms' length.

Paul was a devoted lobster fisherman. Every year, as lobster quotas decreased, he became painfully aware that the line was soon coming to an end. Sitting at the dinner table, Paul gazed grimly at his two sons.

"You boys are most likely the last of the King generation to fish the East Coast waters."

Noah, his mouth full of partially chewed Salisbury steak, nodded his head with a forced saddened expression. He purposely neglected to reveal his plans to break with family tradition, as he thought it would be best to wait until he was old enough to defend his decision. At the age of ten, he could have easily been persuaded to forget his dream. For now, Noah would wait.

ಌ ಌ ಌ

The community's isolation sheltered Noah and his family from such historical events as The Vietnam War and The Peace Movement. His father, a witness to the events, served a tour of duty in Vietnam in 1965, but was shipped home after an unforgiving bullet wreaked havoc with his hip, leaving him with a wooden cane to carry him through life.

"Dad, tell me about 'Nam."

This was at least the sixth time Noah had approached his father on the subject. In the past, whenever he had attempted to ask him about the experience, his father would mechanically shut down. It was now thirty years since his father returned home, so Noah figured that enough time had passed.

He had entered his father's den, a place off-limits to the children, but Noah was feeling particularly brave tonight. Paul was sitting at his desk hunched over a pile of papers, scrutinizing each word. The light from the small desk lamp reflecting off his face showed a tired and strained man. His thick ashen hair, now pallid from the sun's intense rays, revealed gray streaks, making him appear much older.

Noah presumed his father didn't hear him as he continued working uninterrupted. This allowed him a moment to carefully examine the room. The walls, a lush forest green, displayed pictures of famous ships of the past: the *Titanic*, the *Lusitania* and the *Bluenose*. His desk, a glossy oak, contained papers that were neatly stacked and categorized.

Accompanying the desk was a small oak shelf unit, both of which his father had made. The shelves were lined with books on all matters of fishing: boats, equipment, statistical analysis, species of fish, etc. Noah was disappointed.

After a moment of silence, Paul sensed he was no longer alone. He glanced up from the page to find his firstborn staring innocently at him. At the age of eleven, Noah was full of questions too advanced for a young boy to ask. He wanted to sustain his son's innocence for as long as possible, felt that it was his duty…but Noah was making it difficult for him to do so.

"Dad, I want to know about 'Nam."

Looking into those wanting brown eyes, Paul was amazed, as each day went by, how his son was looking more like his mother. He couldn't give him the truth, not now. He would only be a child once.

"Noah, this is not a good time. As you can see, I have a lot of work to do."

On that final remark, Paul returned to his papers. His father never did share his wisdom with Noah. It seemed as though all of the events changing the world were taking place in another country. It could not touch them while his father insisted on keeping it out of the house. Noah assumed his father thought that if he shielded his sons from revolutionary ideas, after a while, the ideas would disintegrate into a pile of ashes. He knew more about human nature than Noah gave him credit for.

Paul had forgotten his son was still standing there, so Noah quietly exited the room. As he headed to his bedroom, his mother gently pulled him aside.

"Noah, your father is a witness to the worst of humanity. He only wants to protect us from the horrors permanently embedded within him."

It was then Noah realized that any knowledge sought on worldly affairs would not be obtained at home. This discovery was the catalyst behind his obsession for the written word.

❧ ❧ ❧

With the arrival of fall came the busy lobster season. The harbor became the focal point of the community's energy. Fishermen and crew tended to their vessels, checking equipment and loading traps, supplies and provisions, their calloused hands reddened by the sting of sea spray. Chatting amongst themselves, they recounted old war stories about their battles with Mother Nature.

On rare occasions, Noah would sit and watch his father and crew recite stories of life on an unforgiving ocean. He observed on each of their faces, including his father's, the battle scars delivered by Mother Nature, each embedded line representing a yarn from a specific trip.

In spite of the beatings they endured, they managed to treasure their livelihood.

Noah's mother had told him that the life of a fisherman was one of the most difficult jobs in the world.

"The fisherman has to enter God's waters, take his creatures, and pray that God will allow him to return home to provide for his family."

Noah stared blankly at her, as his mind was too full of facts to accept the possibility.

Noah and his father barely communicated. Noah had decided a long time ago that they did not have much in common. Although his father was proud of the straight A's he brought home, Noah thought that he might have been a disappointment to him. He believed that he lived in a world separate to his father, outside the world of the fisherman. Paul tried on numerous occasions to include his son in his world, but eventually gave up once he realized Noah had no interest in abandoning his own domain. Noah was content with the arrangement, as keeping their worlds divided was essential for escape.

Paul King expended great effort to keep his boat in the best condition. He spent many hours tending to her needs. In spite of the lame leg, he would passionately sand every inch of her hull by hand, his muscles nearly bursting from the seams of his dingy plaid shirt. On hot days, tiny beads of sweat emerged from his eyebrows, eventually creeping down his rugged face. When he finished sanding, the wood felt as smooth as silk, and when he painted, you would think he was Picasso, each stroke of the brush requiring careful consideration. Noah believed that if the boat could have talked, she would have revealed many secrets about his father.

In keeping with family tradition of naming the boat after the firstborn child, she was appropriately named Noah's Ark. Noah's mother appointed the name, so Noah was obliged to withhold any objections. He was not happy being associated with a Biblical image, but he could never tell his mother, as it would have hurt her tremendously. Noah had learned one important lesson from his father—honor thy mother and father.

Noah's mother, Marta King, is a devout Christian. He suspected that her dedication was an attempt to justify her simple existence, that is, to help her forget the childhood dreams of a life so much different from the one she lived. In those days, if a girl became pregnant at sixteen, she had only one choice: marriage. Once the contract was signed, her destiny was fulfilled.

Marta miscarried twice before giving birth to Aidan. Upon his arrival, he was labeled the miracle child. The two miscarriages affected her deeply, and she submersed herself in the church. Noah assumed that she blamed herself for the miscarriages, and believed by engaging in more church activities, she was doing penance for her supposed sins. She never talked about it, and they never asked. It was as if the events never happened…the silent law.

Marta is a tall woman who carries her height with dignity. Except for her hands, raw and rough from the many hours immersed in soapy dishwater, she is a delicate woman. Her hair, long and gauntly brown, has always been restrained in a tight bun. She could easily be mistaken for a librarian. In earlier years Marta's face, plain but eye-catching, revealed signs of premature aging. Her eyes, weary from numerous hours of uncompensated labor, always bore a gentle light.

Sometimes Noah would catch her methodically peeling potatoes while gazing longingly out the kitchen window across the ocean. He never asked her what she was dreaming about. He just quietly slipped away to his room, as it was not a man's place to ask such questions. It would only create dysfunction in the family unit.

The women of Walden's Cove were blessed with the trying task of ensuring that the men did not stray. Their duty: provide a respectable home for their husbands and children. One of Marta's weekly rituals involved dressing her husband and children in proper religious attire that included clean, pressed black suits complimented by white shirts and black ties. Once she was satisfied with their appearance, she would herd them into the rusted black truck and deliver them to the Divine Sanctuary.

During the hour-long sermons that felt more like a day, Marta sat in deep meditation, forgetting her family beside her. While she was immersed in the minister's words, Aidan, Noah, and her husband shifted awkwardly on the stiff wooden bench.

Noah entertained himself by silently challenging the sermon. His favorites were the songs the congregation sang. For instance, *Jesus loves me this I know, for the Bible tells me so.* Noah wondered what the world would be like if the Bible had said Jesus hated everyone, or if the Bible forgot to mention that Jesus loved everyone. Would everyone still know?

At the end of the service, they would rush home and strip themselves of their sweaty shirts. For the rest of the day they would relish the fact that it would be another seven days until they had to put their church clothes on again.

As a man resistant to change, Paul King managed to maintain his father's attitudes toward women. Before Noah was born, it was decided that he would be the primary financial provider, and Marta would stay at home. She once asked him if she could take a pottery class, but he just laughed and said the classes were for women who had nothing better to do with their time. She did manage to join the Women's Church Group, allowing her to escape for a few hours once a week. Do not misunderstand him. Paul was kind to his wife, respectful of her role in the family unit, and made sure Noah and Aidan were respectful as well.

"Noah, Aidan, thank your mother for this wonderful dinner she worked so hard to make for us," Paul would say after every meal.

Aidan, only five at the time, would giggle and say, "Thank you, Mommy."

Noah, understanding the importance of the gesture, also complied.

ಬಿ ಬಿ ಬಿ

Noah's baby brother, Aidan, was a gem. When he turned six, he transformed into a bundle of energy, bolting around the house in baggy jeans that would end up wrapped around his ankles. His T-shirts carried the residue of everything he ate that day. One of Noah's most gratifying memories was Aidan running through the house screeching, "Run, run as fast as you can, you can't catch me 'cuz I'm the gingerbread man!"

His mother would catch him and lovingly tackle him to the floor, gently nibbling on his shoulder. "You're an awfully sweet gingerbread man," she laughed.

Aidan squealed with delight.

As his older brother, Noah received Aidan's worship. Noah's room was a source of wonderment to him. He spent many hours happily gazing at objects beyond his comprehension. He was mesmerized by the collection of books lining the shelves that stood defiantly against the bedroom walls, scrutinizing the posters of the planets that were strategically placed on every surface.

When Aidan laughed, he shook joyously from head to toe, his scruffy blonde hair bouncing with delight. When his deep blue eyes shone, you could have been blinded. Aidan was, in essence, pure goodness.

Unfortunately, Noah never took the time to appreciate his presence. His biggest regrets in life were the instances that he barred Aidan from his room, so he could be alone with his books. At an early age, solace had been Noah's kindred spirit.

The day Aidan asked Noah how to fly to the Land of Make Believe was the last time that he removed him from his room. Every time Noah reflects on the incident, he is suddenly hurled backwards, the exact date and time permanently scorched in his brain: August 19th, 1995, 2:24 P.M.

Paul was down at the wharf painting the hull of Noah's Ark, while Marta was in the backyard gathering tomatoes for the salad that would accompany that night's meal.

Engrossed in the predator-prey habits of dinosaurs, Noah was not in the mood to entertain a bored six-year-old. He quickly motioned Aidan out the door, rudely closing it behind him. Standing outside Noah's room, Aidan stared at the door. Feeling the tears start to well, his lips starting to quiver, he clenched his fists.

I will show him, he muttered to himself.

Boldly stomping his feet as he headed out the door, he hopped on his cherry-red bicycle and glared at Noah's bedroom window. In mutinous spirit, he embarked on a bike ride without permission, and by doing so, prevented anyone from reminding him to wear a helmet.

As Noah was about to dip into the lost world, he heard the faint jingle of a bike bell. He put the book down on his bed, rose, and peered out the window. He could clearly see Aidan teetering his way down the bumpy dirt road. Although frustrated and annoyed, he decided it would be best that he retrieved him, knowing how his parents would react to his brother's little revolt.

As he turned from the window, he caught a glimpse of Aidan approaching the four-way stop. There were cars at each intersection. He suddenly realized Aidan had not pulled up far enough for all the drivers to see him. What happened next provoked a sort of awakening within Noah. It was not a spiritual awakening, but more like reality walked up and punched him straight in the gut.

Horrified and frozen, he watched his brother cycle straight through the intersection, while the car on the far left also proceeded to drive straight. Standing there a prisoner of time, Noah watched the car collide into Aidan, instantly transforming him into road kill.

Only one thought screamed through his mind: *There is no God.*

Upon that discovery, an unknown survival mechanism switched on and a wall went up around Noah's heart, a wall no person could penetrate. Without it, he would not have been able to weather the days that followed.

Baptism is defined in Webster's Dictionary as *initiating a person into the visible church of Christ*. As an infant, Noah was baptized into his parents' Christian faith. When he was old enough to understand the meaning of the act, he felt betrayed. He realized that as a helpless baby, no one had to worry about him raising his tiny delicate hand and crying out in vain: 'Stop, are you sure this is the right religion? How do you know one of the other religions isn't the true religion?'

In Noah's mind, once baptized, there is no way of reversing the procedure. Sure, you can become skeptical of its beliefs and convert to another religion, but the transparent mark of ownership remains and cannot be burned or scrubbed off. However, Noah did believe he managed to successfully shape the imprint to a design more suited to his personal needs. He was not sure if the design was acceptable to the members of Club Atheist, but it did represent his beliefs. That was all that really mattered.

The old emblem that had embedded itself into Noah's being shifted its shape the moment the car struck Aidan. At the point of impact, an overwhelming wave of self-awareness engulfed him. He became a realist with a new philosophy: A person lives for an undetermined length of time, and if lucky, makes it to a ripe old age, finally ending up a box of bones buried six feet underground. In Noah's mind, a new meaning of life had been born.

ත ත ත

Following Aidan's death, he ceased to exist. One memory standing out in Noah's mind was a comment his mother made at the funeral:

"God is taking care of my baby now."

Without warning, Noah's survival mechanism shifted into high gear, and he felt a rage burst forth. He clenched his fists to refrain from grabbing and shaking his mother, while at the same time demand that she stop fooling herself: *There is no such creature. Stop living in a fantasy world. He is dead, in every way possible.*

But the words never penetrated his lips. Looking into his mother's eyes, all of the anger washed away. All he could do was wrap his arms around her and try to absorb her pain.

The anger Noah experienced may seem cold, but as a card-carrying member of Club Atheist, he felt obliged to honor his membership. He now believed that the way to deal with loss is to accept the loss as a permanent condition. There is no world where a soul travels to spend an eternity in heavenly bliss. If you cannot accept this reality, then you had better go see a shrink who enjoys a challenge, or consume some of that ever-popular brain candy.

❧ ❧ ❧

Life at the King house was never the same after Aidan's death. Paul's character changed tremendously. He plummeted, from a headstrong and logical man to a quiet and reserved creature. When Noah looked into his eyes, he could see there was something missing, perhaps a sense of order.

When it was time for the weekly ritual of preparing for church, Paul no longer put up a fuss, following his wife's instructions to a T. Watching him shave and dress was like watching a robot.

Marta vanished in her religion. Every night after supper, she would sit on the living room sofa and read passages from the Bible, a subdued smile emerging. If Noah did not know better, he would swear she was stoned.

Marta would read to her husband as he sat in his rigid wooden rocking chair staring intently into the fireplace. The warm, red glow reflecting on his face revealed something peculiar about him. It was almost as if he was at peace. Noah was confused, as he couldn't understand how a fantasy could bring such peace. He wanted to enter their sanctuary and ask them, but something inside grabbed and held him back. Instead, he crept to his room.

Noah made the best of his high school years. While the rest of his classmates spent their time hanging out in the smoking area, playing sports and trying to get laid, he took advantage of the knowledge lying at his fingertips. He knew that he needed a scholarship to secure his passage across the causeway, and couldn't afford to take any chances.

He did capture the eye of many of the girls, but the fear of knocking one up kept him cautious. He was not going to be a part of someone else's destiny. If he did become a father, he knew he couldn't leave.

Responsibility—another King trait transferred to the next generation.

By the time Noah reached his senior year, his seat on the honor roll was a permanent fixture. It was time to tell his father the truth.

One early January evening, he entered his father's sanctuary to find him absorbed by the fire. Wrapped in a pink quilt that she had made, his mother rested on the sofa, engrossed in her therapy.

Noah gently seated himself next to her. The anxiety he felt reminded him of an incident that had occurred when he was seven years old. Without his permission, he had taken his father's pocket watch for his class' show and tell, and on the way home he lost it. Fortunately, his mother's presence extinguished the fire, so his punishment entailed spending Saturday mornings loading and unloading lobster traps to pay off the debt. It was important that he learn the value of a dollar. His father's code: If you lost something that did not belong to you, you replaced it. If you broke something, replacing it was not an option. Repairing was the rule, even if it cost less to replace. Reduce, reuse, and recycle was the law in the King home.

Noah had learned only one valuable lesson from the experience: If you applied a fair amount of hand cream to your hands, and wore latex gloves while you slept, you could keep your hands smooth, soft and callous-free.

By clearing his throat, Noah jolted his father out of his dream. Marta looked up from the page and smiled, giving the impression that she knew.

Paul suspiciously eyed his son and said, "You look like you've got somethin' important to say."

Palms sweaty, fidgeting in his seat, Noah replied, "Yeah, I do. It's about my future."

"Your future," Paul said. "That is important."

"As you know," Noah resumed, "this is my senior year in high school."

"Yes."

"And I have been thinking a lot about my future."

Noah suddenly paused with fearful reluctance. His father was staring deeply into his eyes.

"Well, Dad," he managed to stammer, "I'm a man now, so I will be straight with you."

Paul smiled and said, "I expect no less from you, Noah."

"I have decided not to be a lobster fisherman. I want to go to college."

Noah felt an enormous weight ascend from his shoulders. His father returned to the fire and Marta drifted to the page. After what seemed like an eternity of mind-aching silence, Paul turned his head toward his son and gazed tranquilly into his eyes.

"I know."

"You know?" Noah blurted out.

"Yes," he said, "I have known for a long time. Ever since you learned how to read, you plunged into every book you could get your hands on. I realized a long time ago that you were not interested in the lobster business."

"I'm sorry."

Noah felt a strange sensation, but couldn't comprehend it.

"Oh no, don't be sorry. You have big dreams. You want to see the world and learn things that I can't teach you. Noah, as you already said, you are a man now. You have to make your own decisions. Whatever choices you make in life, you have mine and your mother's support."

With that final statement, Paul was consumed by the fire. Marta leaned over, gently kissed her son on the cheek, and returned to her refuge. Noah understood that was his cue to leave.

That was the first and last time Noah and his father communicated in such an intimate way.

Two days after his eighteenth birthday, Noah visited Aidan's muddy grave. Peering into a shallow rain puddle, he tried to create a hallucination of his brother's face—no such luck. A few feet away, he spotted the carcass of a red squirrel and was overcome with the comical urge to bid it farewell, but as a member of Club Atheist that behavior would have been an unforgivable sin.

The following evening, Paul and Marta drove their son to the bus station.

"Be sure to eat meals from all of the food groups," Marta said. "And watch out for strange cults. I saw a story on the TV about cults looking to recruit first-year college students."

Paul laughed, "Now, Marta, the boy ain't gonna get mixed up with those weirdos. He knows better."

Marta turned and looked at her son with fear in her eyes.

Noah smiled. "Dad is right. I know better."

Marta released a relieved smile.

At the bus station, armed with a scholarship, Noah hugged his mother, shook hands with his father, and boarded the bus that would launch him on the path to his destiny.

There were three other passengers neatly spread throughout the bus. Noah took a seat at the back of the bus, needing his privacy; and besides, it was not necessary for everyone to know when he took a leak.

As the bus lurched forward and started to pull out of the station, he settled on the pink and blue flowered seat. His mother would have liked the pattern. Without warning, he was hit with the realization that everything he had been dreaming about for such a long time was now coming true. He took a deep breath and prepared for what he would feel as he watched the town fade away. He turned around and looked directly into his father's eyes, and what he saw shocked him. A tear had rolled down his father's cheek.

Turn around quickly, Noah said to himself. *Keep staring straight ahead. Don't look back. Don't think.*

As the bus crossed the causeway, all of the joy that he imagined he would be filled with did not surface. It felt as though somewhere in his past he had made a really terrible mistake, but he couldn't think about it.

There was no turning back now. Stare straight ahead. Don't look back.

Chapter II

Portland, Maine, was not new to Noah, as he had traveled there many times with his parents. Portland was where civilization began. The town had three times as many streets and houses as Walden's Cove. Aidan would have made a huge haul on Halloween.

Noah was excited, and a little afraid, as The University of Southern Maine was foreign to him. In his youth, he had peered out the window of his father's truck and gazed at the solid stone buildings bearing down upon him. Now, they were not so big, more inviting.

Paul would drive by the school, never giving the buildings and people a second glance, denying Noah the chance to briefly step into the world. All of the different faces were foreign to Noah, only seen in books and magazines. He felt like an alien.

They were lumped together for one purpose: To seek the truth. What truth was, that was still unknown.

༺ ༺ ༺

Noah arrived at the university on a Thursday afternoon. He had decided to give residence life a try, although he didn't have a clue what it would be like. As he walked down the dimly lit hallway, the stench of urine and beer overwhelmed him, and his first drinking experience flashed in his mind. He was sixteen years old and his mother and father had gone to the neighbors' for Friday Bridge Night. Noah broke into his father's liquor cabinet, gotten into the whiskey, and spent the next four hours vomiting his guts up. His father didn't punish him, since spending the evening hanging over the toilet bowl was punishment enough. Also, it was a ritual every young boy went through.

Every dorm room blasted heavy metal music; Noah's ears hurt. Empty beer cans and chip bags scattered the grungy floor. As he approached his room, a stranger emerged. He had long, black, greasy hair, and his eyes were concealed by scraggly bangs. He was wearing faded and torn blue jeans and a T-shirt that bore the slogan, 'I'm with stupid.' There was an arrow below it, pointing to Noah's right.

"Hi," the stranger said. "You must be Noah."

"Yes, I am."

"I'm your roommate, David, but my friends call me Bong Boy."

The aroma emanating from his clothes explained why.

"When you finish unpacking," David said, "a group of us are going to the pub. We want to get an early start. Hey, have you seen all of the fresh tail? Man, I think I've died and gone to heaven. What a party this year is gonna be."

Noah immediately thought about his scholarship. This was all too much for him, and as a former resident of Walden's Cove, he needed time to adjust to the sudden increase in bodies.

৯ ৯ ৯

Noah decided to live in an apartment off-campus. The first place he looked at was convenient, about a five-minute walk from the school. It was located in a house containing six bachelor units. There, he would be alone, but not isolated.

The landlord, Mr. Stubbs, led Noah to the apartment located on the top floor of a three-story house. Mr. Stubbs, a surly old man, heaved and gasped as they made their way up the stairs, his face red and bloated On his tiptoes he stood about five feet six inches, and his belly, protruding from years of beer swilling, hung comfortably over his belt.

When they entered the apartment, Noah discovered that it was not much bigger than his old bedroom. The walls were a glistening white, and if he inhaled deep enough, he could detect a trace whiff of bleach. His mother would have liked it.

"A single bed there," Mr. Stubbs said, pointing to the far right wall. "You can use it as a couch during the day; just take away your pillow."

"Over there," Mr. Stubbs continued as he pointed to the other side of the room, "is your kitchen."

Noah thought that Kitchenette would have been a more appropriate word. It consisted of a small fridge, a stove, and a sink. He would have to use the milk crates he had transported his books in as shelves.

"That there, is the bathroom." Mr. Stubbs pointed to a door adjacent to the kitchenette. The wall behind the kitchenette separated the apartment from the bathroom.

"I'll take it."

৯ ৯ ৯

Entering his first year, Noah had no idea what he wanted to be, making it difficult to pick a major. To discover what subject appealed to him, he decided to enroll in a number of science and liberal arts classes. He dove into Biology, Psychology, Philosophy, English, and Anthropology, and found himself thriving in the environment. There was so much knowledge within the walls of the school; it was his idea of heaven.

The one course that captured his attention was Biology. He loved learning about the planet and the history of its inhabitants. It fascinated him to learn how humans evolved. He found himself agreeing with some scientists, and disagreeing with others. He needed to know more.

Noah decided to major in Biological Science, but evolution was not the only subject that fascinated him. The evolution of the human mind and its thought processes was an alluring mystery. He became obsessed with human nature, and yearned to discover the absolute truth about his existence.

He absorbed himself in the search, from Charles Darwin to Carl Sagan. His test scores and research papers impressed the hell out his instructors, and to his surprise, he found his calling—a teacher, a mentor.

So what knowledge will I pass on to my future protégés? Noah asked himself.

⁓⁓⁓

He conveyed that question to his academic advisor, Daniel Lowenstein.

For a man assigned to assist students with fulfilling their destinies, Mr. Lowenstein was not what he expected.

His office was located at the end of the hallway on the second floor of the administration building. As Noah entered the room, he quickly gathered as much information about Mr. Lowenstein as he could. The piles of books haphazardly scattered along the shelves jumped out at him, as there was no logical order to them; alphabetizing them would have been an improvement. His desk was cluttered with papers. Noah was not sure how he managed to get through each day.

Mr. Lowenstein was wearing faded blue jeans, accompanied by a black sports jacket covering a black T-Shirt. His hair, long and gray, was tied in a ponytail. Noah wondered if he was looking at the remnants of the 1960's.

"So Noah, have you found your ideal career yet?"

"I think so. I want to be a teacher, preferably a university professor."

"I see. What subjects are you interested in teaching?"

"That's my problem," Noah replied. "I'm fascinated with human nature. I mean, with what makes people tick, but I realize that there are many different fields pertaining to this subject. I feel that if I major in one subject, I may not discover the absolute truth about human nature."

"Interesting," Mr. Lowenstein murmured as he leaned back in his chair, gently stroking his chin.

"You see," Noah continued, "everyone knows a lot about one thing, and a little about other things. How can I learn about one aspect of human nature, while knowing nothing about the others? Don't you think I would be passing on nothing to my students?"

"Hmm," he said, "I think you are looking to accomplish something more than just passing on your knowledge to a classroom of students. It sounds like you are interested in discovering the meaning of life, The Holy Grail."

"Well," Noah laughed, "I'm an atheist. I want to know the truth about our existence, the truth with the evidence to support it. To do this, I have to cover a lot of different areas. God is not a part of the equation."

"Let me understand what you are saying…you want to combine the knowledge about all aspects of human nature to discover how you came to be?"

"Yes."

Noah wondered if he was impressed with his maturity.

"And you want to pass this information onto others."

"Yes."

"So…" he pauses, perhaps looking for a sign of anticipation.

"You want to write a book," he announces.

A book, Noah thought in wonderment. Writing a book had never crossed his mind.

"Yes, a book," Noah shouted, "that's perfect. You see, so much evil has been committed in God's name, I feel that if I write a book proving his existence is a myth, people will no longer be able to justify their cruel acts. It's my belief that humanity would be better off without a God. God not only has been used to justify evil acts, he also gives a false sense of reality, that is, no matter how bad the world is, there is a place waiting for them that will put an end to their unhappiness. I think if people stopped believing in God, they would be more prone to try to make their lives better. I really believe I could make a wonderful contribution to mankind."

Noah stopped, in shock at the words that just fell out of his mouth. It was the first time he actually informed someone of his plans. He felt his face start to burn.

"That's awfully generous of you."

Noah detected a hint of sarcasm but dismissed it as not knowing him.

"I agree," Mr. Lowenstein continued, "that before writing such a book, you really should look at all aspects of human nature. This would include the biological, sociological, and psychological aspects of the human mind. I would advise that you major in the biological sciences, but make sure you take courses in the humanities that deal with this subject. Then, if you wish, you can further your studies by taking a Masters Degree, followed by a Doctorate Degree. You will be able to earn a living by teaching, and write a book at the same time."

Noah's future was now written, his destiny packed in a nutshell, his flight plan filed. He was focused on his goal and determined to succeed. He was going to change the world; change the course of evolution.

Looking back at the strength of his convictions many years later, one thought always crosses his mind: *Beware of false prophets.*

෴ ෴ ෴

During the next four years, Walden's Cove, along with his parents, faded to a distant memory. Noah only returned home for the Christmas holidays. For some strange reason, he felt compelled to be home on December twenty-fifth.

When he did return home, it was as though he had been gone for years. As the rickety bus stumbled across the causeway, he waited for the anticipated feelings of separation; there were none. He assumed that it would take time for the separation process to take place.

When the bus pulled into the station, Noah peered out of the frosted window to see his parents huddled in the cold, the warm steam rising from their chapped lips. As he stepped off the bus, Marta wrapped her arms tightly around her son.

"Are you getting enough to eat?" she asked while squeezing his ribs.

"Now, Marta," Paul laughed, "you're gonna squeeze the life right outta the boy."

The house was always how Noah expected it to be, nothing new. His presence added life to the surroundings. Marta sat her son down on the sofa and made him report every detail of his experience at the university. His father remained silent, listening attentively.

After the holidays, Marta and Paul drove their son to the bus station.

Loaded with homemade squares—raisin and peanut, Noah's favorite—he boarded the bus. This time, when he looked back into his father's eyes, he saw something different: sadness mixed with contentment. It was not until many years later that he learned his father had stopped sharing sea stories with his crew, but instead recited stories about his son at the big college.

ᛣ ᛣ ᛣ

Noah worked at the university during the summer months, employed in various departments that included the library, as well as a research assistant for university professors. The opportunity allowed him to explore other areas of human nature that he was unable to take during his regular course schedule. He basically became a walking and talking encyclopedia.

He logged many hours in the library, making it a second home. The clerk would find him huddled at a desk, surrounded by dusty books. He was always the last to leave, and needed reminding when it was closing time.

Noah's social life was practically nonexistent. His friends consisted of the individuals within his study group. There were many who tried on numerous occasions to entice him to the Thursday Pub Night at the university, but he would remember his scholarship and decline the offer. It was important that he stay focused.

Once in a while, Noah met an interesting woman, but she soon grew bored with him when he neglected to give her his undivided attention. There would be plenty of time for recreation once the diploma was firmly in hand.

ᛣ ᛣ ᛣ

By the time Noah reached the first term of his graduate program, he had acquired such a vast amount of knowledge, he comically thought his brain had reached maximum capacity. He had carefully followed his academic advisor's instructions, and graduated with a major in Biology. He took a number of courses relating to human nature and even set aside his dislike for organized religion, taking classes focusing on such theories as *The First Cause*—everything has a cause, and the first cause of everything is God.

To balance the philosophical aspects of religion, he enrolled in classes dealing with the function of religion in society. To his horror, he discovered that there were many more atrocities committed against Man in the name of God than he had once thought. Every time he uncovered an atrocity, he would remember his mother's commitment to the fictitious creature, becoming more determined to complete his mission. He sincerely believed that worshipping this creature would eventually lead to the downfall of humanity, and he was not about to let that happen.

ᛣ ᛣ ᛣ

It was the fall of Noah's first semester of graduate school when he first learned a valuable lesson about creating your own destiny: destiny sometimes has a mind of its own, and can be ruthless to those attempting to control it.

Noah considers himself a survivor of Destiny's wrath.

One late-night phone call decisively altered his destiny. The path that he created and diligently followed was destroyed in an instant, and along with the destruction flowed the disintegration of reality as he had come to understand it.

This is the second of two dates permanently burned in Noah's mind. The fateful day: September 20th, 1995, 11:32 P.M. Noah was sitting on his bed, leafing through mounds of material, looking for any information that would help support his quest. He had decided to get an early start on his thesis paper, since he planned to turn the paper into a book someday. He had already picked a catchy title, *How I Got Here and Where I am Going*, and was currently bouncing around some ideas.

There was an intense rainstorm pounding on his window. Without warning, his search was interrupted by the startling ring of the telephone. On the other end of the line were panic and pain—his mother. The terror in her voice wielded him backward in time to a place that forever haunted him, Aidan's demise. He was overcome with a feeling of nausea.

His father had ceased to exist. Noah's Ark and her crew perished amidst a furious storm. Marta could only repeat one phrase to her son: "I am all alone. I am so alone."

Feeling as if a knife had been driven into his heart, he managed to reply: "No, Mom, I am here. I am coming home."

The next moments were a blur, as Noah had only been able to put together bits and pieces of the events that followed.

He found himself running through the vicious bullets of rain that pelted his back. At the time, he was involved with a girl who had her own car. Her name was Rebecca Holt, and they had been seeing each other for about six weeks. She was a physics major in the final year of her undergraduate program. Noah will always remember Rebecca as the one who introduced him to the work of Stephen Hawking.

Rebecca was different from the other girls Noah had dated. She talked to him, not at him, and the relationship was starting to become more than just sex for him. He enjoyed being around her. She challenged him.

Completely drenched, Noah desperately pounded on Rebecca's apartment door. When she opened it, he stood there like a drowned rat. He wanted to fall into her delicate arms, but restrained himself.

"What are you doing?" Rebecca cried. "You are soaked, come in."

"I can't," Noah stammered. "My mother…my father…I have to go home. I need your car."

"What? You can't drive all the way home in this weather. It's too dangerous."

"Please," Noah begged, "my father is dead. My mother needs me. I need her."

Rebecca gazed into Noah's eyes and witnessed something that she had never seen there before—helplessness. In spite of her objections, Noah secured the keys, and in record time, he was on the road. Rebecca never saw Noah again.

ைக ைக ைக

The rain was merciless that night, hammering the windshield with a blind rage. The steam rising from the hood allowed Noah to see only a few feet in front of him. In spite of Mother Nature's efforts, he plowed on, unaware of the danger that lie ahead.

As the car fearlessly pushed through the sheets of water, he suddenly noticed an object blocking his path. It looked to be frozen in time. To his best recollection, it was a moose. Noah slammed on the brakes and his hands took on a life of their own. He felt the car slide, and in less than a second, he was hurtling down a steep embankment.

Noah covered his eyes. That was his last memory in the car.

The Sinking of Noah's Ark

Chapter III

As a child, Noah was taught that when one dies, there is a long tunnel with a brilliant light at the end of it. No one knows what happens when you go through the light, but it is assumed heaven is on the other side. Noah imagined that it was a place much like McDonalds Playland. As the years went by, he realized it was unlikely that Mayor McCheese and Grimace were on the other side waiting to embrace him.

Where Noah actually ended up was as far from the glorious afterlife as one can get. His last memory as he toppled down the hill was shielding his eyes, with no final thoughts or regrets, just darkness. When he uncovered his eyes, he found himself in the last state he expected to be in—alive.

After a brief period of confusion, Noah managed to pull himself together. He looked around to find himself in a foreign room. Upon careful examination of his surroundings, he realized that it was a courtroom.

He was not familiar with the courtroom, as it lacked any features identifying it with any known justice system. There were no flags of countries, no pictures of presidents or monarchs. Except for a luminous coat of faded gray paint, the walls were completely bare. When studying the walls, he could have sworn there was white trying to force its way through.

Noah discovered that he was sitting in the witness chair. It was wooden, with a red velvet-cushioned seat. To the left of his seat was the jury box, but no jurors were present. The judge's bench was located to his immediate right, but no judge presided. In front of the judge's box was either the defense or prosecutor's table and it too was empty. Directly in front of him, he noticed another table, which he also believed to be either the prosecutor or defense table. The only difference here was the presence of a man seated at the table, looking down at a pile of papers. What was so startling about the man was that Noah was sure he was not there when he first opened his eyes.

After a moment of dreadful silence, the man proceeded to push his chair out, stand, and slowly walk toward him. As each shoe scuffed the bare wooden floor, a low, intense echo was released. A shifty smile materialized.

The stranger was wearing a long black robe, completed by a pair of shiny, black shoes. His hair, jet black and combed back on his head, revealed a distinct receding hairline. His facial features looked as if they had been perfectly chiseled from fine stone. There were few signs of aging, but Noah guessed by the distinguished aura surrounding him that he was about fifty.

As the man approached, his eyes grabbed hold of Noah's eyes. He had never seen eyes so dark before. They were as black as coal. When looking into them, it was as though he was looking at nothing; the darkness stretched on forever. Noah could not speak. He could only stare foolishly at his menacing smile.

When he reached an area about a foot and a half in front of Noah, he stopped abruptly. Without taking his eyes off him, the stranger slowly opened his mouth and began to speak.

"You, Noah Paul King, have been brought to the highest court in the universe, at my request, to tell your truth, and nothing but your truth, so help your God."

His hollow, gruff voice hammered like the final nail driven into a coffin.

He paused, and his smile transformed into a devious grin, revealing a distinct set of pearly white teeth. Noah stared in complete bewilderment.

After a moment of desperate search, Noah seized his voice.

"Ah, okay."

Without warning, the man erupted in a fit of laughter.

"Okay? Is that all you have to say?"

Noah wiped his sweaty forehead with his shirtsleeve. The stranger grinned, enjoying his anxiety.

"Well, I'm puzzled," Noah replied.

"I bet you are," he laughed.

"I have no idea where I am, and what I am being charged with, and..."

"Wait," the stranger interrupted, "it's the 'Your God' thing, isn't it?"

"Yes."

This has got to be some sort of hallucination, Noah thought.

"I can eliminate your confusion simply," he said. "First of all, you are not on trial. You are here as a witness for the Defense. Secondly, it is I, the Prosecutor, assigned to the trial. And thirdly—this is the best part..."

By now, the man was snickering devilishly.

"You know the term God, that is used to identify the Creator?"

Noah was not sure if he was asking him a question or making a statement. Feeling the dampness behind his neck grow cold, he answered with a blunt, "Yes."

"Well," the man said, "I am pleased to inform you that this higher being does in fact exist. You are here not only as a witness, but also as evidence of His creation. You have been assigned with the delightful task of defending Him."

Staring intently into his eyes, Noah felt as though he was just caught with his pants down.

After a moment of gathering his thoughts, Noah was overcome with the realization that everything he believed in for such a long time was instantly annihilated—road kill.

With all the vast knowledge he had acquired over the years, only one futile thought emerged: *Oops.*

"Well, Noah," the stranger laughed, "this must be an overwhelming experience for you, but I do not have the time, nor the patience, to wait for you to fall down on your knees and cry out Praise the Lord, Hallelujah."

What a sarcastic fellow, Noah chuckled to himself. *I like this guy.*

He took a deep breath and mentally exerted immense self-control.

"Am I dead?"

The man smiled, and without warning, lifted his right hand and slapped Noah across the face.

"Ouch! Why the hell did you do that?"

"Do you feel dead, Noah?" he laughed.

"No," he replied, not knowing what being dead was supposed to feel like.

"Well," he snorted, "then you're not dead."

"Where am I?" Noah asked.

"You have been brought to the fork in the road. Which path you take—that is, whether you return your reality or cease to exist—all depends on the verdict."

Trying to appear calm, Noah asked how God could be put on trial.

"That is a good question, my monotheistic friend. God is on trial because He has allowed himself to be put on trial. You see, a long time ago, God handpicked a select few to be watchers over the human evolution process. They are called the *Guardians of the Light*. For years, the Guardians have been watching the decline of your planet, and its species. Several of the Guardians have asked God to take action, resulting in this trial, and you are here to refute the charges filed against God."

Charges...this is insane, Noah whispered to himself. *This cannot be real.*

"And as to the charges," the man relentlessly continued, "God has been charged with committing the greatest crime of all: As an all-knowing, all-powerful, and all-good being, he knowingly created evil and allowed it to flourish. This evil, as you well know, is the human being."

He paused, and roared with laughter. "Isn't it about time?"

Noah was floored, and for the first time in his life, completely terrified. He has just found himself face-to-face with the impossible. Moisture started to fill his palms.

"If God is found guilty," the stranger said, "human life on Earth will cease to exist. All that will remain are the species you refer to as inferior, the plant and animal life. If found innocent, the human evolution process will continue on its merry way."

Dazed, Noah rubbed his eyes, struggling to make sense of what was happening.

"Okay, let me try to understand what you are suggesting. God is the alleged criminal. He created Man, which is a crime because of the evil Man has inflicted on his species, as well as the other species. My job is to show that the creation of Man was not intended to be an evil deed. This will prove that Man is not an evil product of God's Creation, and by doing so, I will save the human race?"

The fiendish grin revealed itself again.

"By George," he bellowed, "I think he's got it."

"But why me? I have dedicated my life to proving God is a myth."

"That's why you are the perfect choice. You have dedicated your life to making sense of human nature. By acquiring so much knowledge on the subject, you have the power to prove His innocence."

He paused, and in a deep harsh voice said, "But I warn you now, I do not think this can be done. I believe I have an open-and-shut case."

"So if you are here to end human life on earth, then you must be the Devil."

Noah can't believe he just asked such a question.

The man burst into a laugh so powerful, Noah had to grip his seat to keep from toppling over.

"I like that," he managed to say. "You are definitely the right man for the job. I am well aware that your species likes to attach labels to everything, so to make your stay more comfortable, since I am the prosecutor assigned to the trial, you may call me Prosecutor."

That's original, Noah thought.

"Okay, Prosecutor, so where is God? Should he not be here for his own trial?"

"Oh, his presence is not required at this time," he said. "I plan to spend a lot of time in debate with you. Once I have finished, God will be summoned."

Noah paused and glanced around the room. He thought it was strange that they were the only two in the room.

"If you are the Prosecutor, then who is the Judge?"

"Why, that would be the most impartial judge in the universe…Time."

"Time? How can Time be a judge? Time isn't an intellectual life form."

"Noah, you are thinking too much in terms of the physical. Open your mind. Time is an element that cannot be controlled or manipulated. Time has no biases. You cannot touch, taste, hear or smell time, but it's always there, always constant. The process of how time unfolds depends on how one makes use of it. Once you have provided your defense, only then will Time reveal the verdict."

"Okay," Noah said, "who will read the verdict?"

"Five Guardians have been selected to be on the jury. They will listen to each of our arguments, and at the end of the trial they will find God guilty or innocent. Their verdict will favor the one who gives the best argument. The Guardians will not address the court; they will only listen carefully to our words."

"Where are they?"

"Are you blind, man?" Prosecutor laughed as he pointed to the jury box.

Noah glanced to his left, and his jaw dropped. As if appearing out of nowhere, five men and women sat in the jury box wearing white robes, their faces lacking emotion.

"This can't be real," Noah stutters.

"Do you need another slap?" Prosecutor asked.

"I don't know."

Prosecutor chuckled. "I believe you are familiar with each member of the jury."

He walked over to the jury box and stood in front of the first person.

"I will now introduce you to them."

He pointed to the man sitting in front of him.

"Noah, meet Stephen Biko."

The man glanced at Noah, nodding.

"Mr. Biko fought to end apartheid in South Africa. In August of 1977, Mr. Biko was arrested for the last time and severely beaten by police. He went into a coma and died within a month of his arrest."

Prosecutor moved to the next juror, "Noah, meet John Humphrey."

Mr. Humphrey nodded.

"Mr. Humphrey was a leading author of the *Universal Declaration of Human Rights*. He also helped establish *Amnesty International Canada* and the *Canadian Human Rights Foundation*. He spent his life devoted to the advocacy of human rights. He died during this past year that you call 1995."

Prosecutor moved to the third person.

"Noah, meet Albert Einstein. Mr. Einstein is famous for his work as a scientist, especially his *Theory of Relativity* and the *Quantum Theory*. As a scientist, he fought for international disarmament. He became well known for his efforts concerning social causes. Mr. Einstein died in 1955."

He moved to the fourth person.

"Noah, this is Dian Fossey. Ms. Fossey spent twenty-two years studying wild mountain gorillas in Africa. In 1985, she was murdered in reprisal for her efforts to stop the poaching of gorillas and other animals in Africa."

He moved to the fifth and final jury member.

"Noah, this is Sitting Bull. Sitting Bull was a Native American leader of the Sioux tribe. He led the fight against efforts of the United States Government to take his people's lands and put them on reservations. He was arrested by the US Army in 1890 and murdered in a gunfight while in custody.

Once Prosecutor finished his introductions, he walked over and stood in front of Noah. Noah didn't notice him; his eyes were still on the jury. He was in awe; it was as if each had been magically taken out of the pictures he had seen of them.

"Noah, snap out of it. There's a lot riding on this trial."

Noah turned his head toward Prosecutor.

"Okay, sorry," he replied. "But there's one other statement that you made earlier puzzling me."

"And that would be?"

"Well, in your opening statement you made a reference to *your Truth*. I'm not sure what you mean by this phrase."

"Ah," Prosecutor laughed, "you are not required to tell me the truth, only your truth."

"But isn't truth absolute?"

"Whose truth are you talking about, Noah? Your mother's, your father's, or your dentist's?"

"Okay, then will my truth be the absolute truth?"

"Are you all-knowing, Noah?" He sneered.

"No, of course not."

"So how can it be the absolute truth?"

"I guess it can't be, but if I reveal my truth, and it's not the absolute truth, how can I prove God's innocence? I mean, what is the point of revealing my truth?"

"The point is simple," he laughed. "Your truth depends on how much you want to live."

"Okay," Noah said. "I will not tell you how things are, but how I perceive things to be. I have to do this knowing that my truth will be different from how many others of my species perceives the truth. For instance, a bartender in Australia or a hairstylist in England may perceive the truth in a different manner. It will be how well I present my truth that is the critical component that will either convict God or find him innocent."

"Exactly," Prosecutor said. "At the end of the trial you will leave here either as a liar, or as one hell of a storyteller."

෴ ෴ ෴

Settling into his seat, Noah mentally prepared to match wits with his opponent. If they each had a fiddle, it would have been a momentous occasion, one for the history books.

Prosecutor cleared his throat and began to address the court.

"Before I begin examining the witness, I would like to open with a statement that has been passed down from generation to generation throughout the history of mankind."

Prosecutor paused and flashed a quick wink in Noah's direction.

"In the beginning," he declared, "God created the heavens, the earth and…"

Prosecutor suddenly collapsed in a frenzy of laughter. Noah found himself liking this guy even more.

Struggling to compose himself, Prosecutor looked at the Jury.

"I beg the court's forgiveness," he said, "but I have always found that line to be a great opener."

The Jury smiled.

Prosecutor turned to Noah, his smile vanishing, and his eyes closing to a squint.

"Do you, Noah Paul King, acknowledge and accept the higher power?"

Glancing around the room Noah said, "Well considering my situation, I suppose that I do."

"Do you acknowledge the power as the Creator of the world you reside on?"

"Yes."

Again, Noah could not believe he was saying this.

"And this being is what you refer to as God?"

"Yes."

"Good," he said. "I would like it entered into the record that, for the purpose of this trial, the Creator will be identified as God, and the gender will be assigned as male. By doing so, it will prevent any confusion on the part of the witness, as those are the terms he associates with the Creator. Now, I will begin my debate with the witness."

"Wait," Noah interrupted. "I would like to enter into the record the fact that I have never met God and may be lacking some important information about Him."

"Request denied," Prosecutor snapped. "All you need to know is that God exists."

"That's it?"

It couldn't be just that, Noah thought. *After everything that was said and written about God, to have him summed up so neatly.* He at least expected a drum roll or a big cymbal clash.

"Yes, that's it." Prosecutor said. "There is no deep mystery to Him. He is the simplest of all life forms, and the easiest to understand. He is the Creator of the universe, and he is all-knowing, all-good, and all-powerful. That is all you need to know. Now, let's move on."

"Okay," Noah mumbled.

He was starting to feel a gnawing sensation in the pit of his stomach.

Prosecutor closed his eyes and crossed his arms, appearing to be meditating or collecting his thoughts. He was a pale man with noticeably translucent knuckles. Noah wondered if he would open his eyes and brandish a huge set of fangs.

After a few moments, he slowly opened his eyes and stared into Noah's. This made him uncomfortable, but he tried not to show it, believing that it wouldn't be a good idea to reveal weakness this early in the game.

"I will now enter the witness, Noah Paul King, into evidence. Mr. King's physical presence is living proof of God's willful creation. I will provide a factual account exposing the life form sitting here before the court as the evil product of God's creation."

"I object," Noah shouted. "A person can't be entered into evidence."

"Have you forgotten whose courtroom you are in?" Prosecutor laughs. "I thought by now you would have realized that the rules of your world don't apply here. Your objection is over ruled."

Feeling like a complete goof, Noah could only stare back at him. What could he say? He was in uncharted waters.

"Now," Prosecutor said. "Back to business."

Business, Noah stewed under his breath. *This is definitely not business.*

"The Prosecution will prove that God knowingly created a species responsible for inflicting pain and suffering on each other, as well as the other species inhabiting the planet. By creating such an evil and allowing it to flourish, God, an all-knowing and all-good being, committed the greatest sin possible; therefore, he is responsible for their evil acts. This is a violation of everything he embodies, so in order to right this wrong, God must be found guilty, and his creation eliminated. By doing so, God will reclaim the force of goodness by allowing the remaining species on earth to live free of the evil now threatening their existence, as well as the planet's existence."

He stopped and beamed with pride, his lips curling into a taunting grin.

Force of Goodness, Noah thought. *Since when am I in a Star Wars movie?*

"I will now explain the format of the trial," Prosecutor said. " I will be presenting a series of arguments, and providing evidence that will prove the creation of humans was an evil act. It is your responsibility to prove..."

The fiendish smile surfaced again.

"Well... to prove it isn't so. But remember, you are here to defend God. The fate of humanity rests on the words you speak. Are you ready?"

Noah felt his heart racing.

"Do I have a choice?"

"Nope," he replied cheerfully.

Noah wondered if this was how a drowning victim felt when he was about to submit to his fate.

Prosecutor cleared his throat and said, "I will now begin at the witness' beginning. In order to understand God's Creation, we have to first understand how his Creation came into existence. By doing so, I will quickly and effectively prove God's guilt."

His smug confidence made Noah squirm.

"The human scientist," he began, "has been on an everlasting quest to discover how the universe came to be. The human is a curious animal, always looking for the hidden truth; that is, the absolute truth explaining how he came to exist in such a vast and astounding universe. One impressive story is the tale of Stephen Hawking's *The Big Bang*. Are you familiar with this story, Noah?"

"Yes, proponents of *The Big Bang* theory suggest that the universe erupted from a hot dense ball of matter and energy that burst and expanded evenly in all directions."

"Exactly," Prosecutor said, "after a long period of time, the matter cooled, and after another lengthy period of time, temperatures were cool enough for celestial objects to form: that is, the sun, stars...etcetera. Billions of years later, the result is the evidence now sitting before me, living proof of God's creation.

"Noah, you sit here today aware of God's existence. You also accept God as the catalyst behind the explosion resulting in the birth of the universe. By accepting this fact, I contend that God is responsible for creating humans, and since God is the Creator of human life, He is also responsible for the evil and suffering resulting from His creation."

Prosecutor abruptly stopped, turned, walked to his table, and seated himself.

"So," he triumphantly grinned, "is it time for the verdict to be read?"

Prosecutor is full of himself, Noah thought. *I may be able to use it to my advantage later on.*

"No," Noah laughed, "I won't make it that easy for you. You may not be aware of this, but I'm not one to back down from a challenge that quickly."

"Aha," Prosecutor roared, "a battle, I think that I'm going to enjoy this."

I am glad he is, he thought. *I would rather go back to the car.*

"Okay," Noah said. "Your argument is entirely too simplistic and I believe that I can poke holes in it, and cast reasonable doubt."

He unexpectedly stopped, as he had forgotten that he was in a foreign courtroom.

"If I provide reasonable doubt, will God be found innocent?"

Prosecutor's jackal-like smile emerged.

"Yes, like your justice system, our arguments have to be convincing."

"That's a relief," Noah sighed.

Prosecutor slipped his hands behind his head and leaned back in his chair, stretching his legs outward.

"Well," he said, "carry on."

"I agree," Noah began, "that so far, science has proven *The Big Bang Theory* to be the most credible theory explaining how the universe was created. One example of the evidence that scientists provide is the stars and other celestial objects are continually moving away from Earth. I agree with the theory stating that universe and time, as humans have come to understand it, had a beginning, and it is estimated that this beginning took place approximately fifteen billion years ago.

"The scientists also suggest that there is another plane of reality existing outside our own known reality, and it is believed that this alternate space/time plane is where the universe erupted from. Scientists have not been able to discover this plane because they say it is presently outside man's known laws of physics. Some theologians believe God resides in this alternate plane of existence. If I wasn't sitting in this courtroom right now, I would strongly disagree with them, but either way you look at it, neither theory has been proven to be absolute. It has been left to the individual to decide."

"And you, Noah," Prosecutor interjected, "chose science as the ultimate explanation."

"Yes, I was a believer in the tangible, the logical. There was no physical evidence proving that there was a Creator."

Laughing, Prosecutor remarked, "Ah yes, the need to see, hear, touch, taste, and smell. The need to grasp it in both hands. Anyway, I digress. Please continue."

"Any way you look at it, you can argue that the universe was created about fifteen billion years ago. Now, Man appeared on the planet approximately four million years ago. If I do my math correctly, this means that the universe existed approximately fourteen billion, nine hundred and ninety-six million years before Man arrived. If God was so determined to create the universe for Man, then why would he have designed it so that it took so long for Man to appear? Why didn't he do it in an instant, or in six days, like the Bible says? I believe I have the answer."

Prosecutor straightened his back and slid his hands under his chin, allowing his elbows to rest on the table.

"And what may that answer be?"

His sarcasm shook Noah's confidence. He believed that was his plan.

"It's my argument that God didn't directly create Man. Man is the product of the process of evolution. He was not specifically created to rule the universe. Since there are millions of species on the Earth, it would be illogical for God to create a species to rule all other species. It is also illogical for a being of all-goodness to commit an act of tyranny, since tyranny cannot exist in such a being.

"Let's pose, for example, that although I don't have any physical evidence of hominid life forms on other planets, we are not the only planet possessing life."

"You aren't talking about little green creatures obsessed with your species' rectums, are you? Prosecutor asked.

"No," Noah chuckled, feeling his cheeks grow warm.

"Well that's good," he said. "I definitely have no desire to understand that pattern of thinking."

"I will try to provide a logical defense."

"Good," Prosecutor laughed. "I don't want this trial turning into a circus. Please continue."

"In recent years, there has been evidence discovered indicating that life may exist outside of our solar system. If life has occurred here, around an ordinary star in an ordinary galaxy, could it have not appeared somewhere else? Should we not expect life to be a natural event?

"In fact, scientists have recently found strong evidence suggesting that primitive life may have existed on Mars more than 3.6 billion years ago. So, if primitive life forms did exist off our planet, is it not totally inconceivable to think there may be other life forms out there? We have not yet achieved the technology to travel great distances to find out exactly what is out there. It is also limited of Man to think that such a vast universe contains only one planet of life forms."

"True," Prosecutor said. "I suppose Christopher Columbus straightened many people out."

"Yes, he did; therefore, the possibility of life existing somewhere out there infers the illogic of thinking the universe was created for Man, and Man alone. I argue that it was God's intention to create a universe where millions, and perhaps billions, of species could live. Man is just one of those species: an obscure molecule in a vast ocean."

"So," Prosecutor interrupts, "you are arguing that God started the process, but does not control it?"

"Yes, I'm arguing that it was never intended to be controlled. For example: picture the starting line of a huge marathon. The person firing the pistol is responsible for starting the race, but the moment the pistol is fired, he no longer plays a role. What happens during the race depends on the individuals in it, and their actions affect the outcome. So to conclude, Man is just a mere product of the evolutionary process. Therefore, God cannot be found guilty on this argument alone."

"From what you have argued so far," Prosecutor said, " Man could ask himself the following question: Is there any virtue left within that would help lift me from this self-constructed pedestal I now sit upon?"

"Yes, that about sums up my argument."

Noah was feeling damn good. Triumphant would be a more appropriate word. He looked into Prosecutor's eyes for any sign of defeat, but saw nothing.

"Well," Prosecutor said, "you held your own, but I would not get too cocky. We have a long way to go. That was just round one."

※ ※ ※

Prosecutor rose from his seat and slowly paced back and forth in front of Noah, the irritating scuff gnashing on his nerves. He had the feeling Prosecutor was about to annihilate him.

After a moment, Prosecutor halted in his tracks and glared abrasively at him. He was ready for round two.

"In order to understand the essence of human nature," Prosecutor began, "I have to go back to the beginning of the tangible, that is, the beginning of life as Man understands it. I'm referring to the process of evolution as it relates to living creatures, and how the process resulted in the creation of modern Man. I believe you pointed out earlier that God is the Creator of the process of evolution, and Man is the result of the process. So, I will now tell you the story of Man."

The slick smile re-emerged.

"Evolution," Prosecutor said, "refers to changes in the gene frequency of a population over a long period of time. Evolution occurs because *different individuals, who are genetically different, tend to leave different numbers of offspring to grow, mature and reproduce in the next generation.* As this process is repeated from generation to generation, there is a change in the genetic structure of the population. Evolution is more likely to be successful when a species is isolated and presented with new survival challenges. The environment provides a high death rate, thereby filtering out the weak. Scientists believe that the first hominid, the walking ape, arrived this way. Would you not agree?"

"Yes," Noah replied, "there is more to it, but you cited the gist of it."

Prosecutor laughed. Noah thought about disagreeing with him to see his reaction, but decided against it, as he must not forget the seriousness of the situation.

"Although the scientists don't know the exact time this happened," Prosecutor continues, "it is believed that a small group of primates was the predecessor to the historical event. As the climate experienced changes across Africa, forests began to vanish. The shortage of food forced the tree dwellers to the ground. There were now new predators in their midst. If they were to survive, they would have to work together.

"The first hominid, *Ardipitheus Ramidus*, had trouble surviving. The women had difficulty raising children while searching for food. Life was brutal and the death rate fierce. Ramidus decided it would be best to settle in one place, ensuring his offspring survived. The community was born. As the society grew, food became scarce so many left in search of food. Communities were now being established all over the place. The agriculturist was now on the scene."

Prosecutor paused and eyed Noah suspiciously.

"Have I omitted any critical point in the story of your evolution so far?"

"No," Noah replied, "you are providing an orderly summary."

Prosecutor smiled, giving the impression that he was pleased with himself.

"As the evolutionary process continued," Prosecutor said, "Man's quality of tools and weapons improved, and as the population increased, so did competition for food. His culture was now more complicated, one that required intellect and language. Thus, *Homo habilis*, maker of fire for cooking, heat, and keeping predators at a safe distance, made his entrance.

"About 1.8 million years ago, *Homo erectus* entered the stage. He was a warrior, hunter, inventor and explorer. During the two million years of Homo erectus, tribes were small and isolated. Within each tribe, genetic and social differences evolved, each developing their own style of behavior, dress, customs and speech.

"About 300,000 years ago, *Homo sapiens* appeared on the world stage, the result of almost four million years of evolution. Man was now the product of millions of deaths and hardships, only the strongest and most cunning survived."

Prosecutor paused and gazed into his eyes. Noah clenched his hands together in his lap, as the critical part of Prosecutor's argument was fast approaching.

"About 120,000 years ago, modern Man arrived on the scene. From that point on, Man's creative mind enslaved other animals, and even others of his own species. He perpetrated the most horrific acts ever committed by any species. He exterminated his foes ruthlessly, often in large numbers, and greedily consumed the world around him, ravaging those weaker than he and inevitably leaving them to die."

Prosecutor stopped and looked thoughtfully towards Noah, who looked down in his lap, feeling that Prosecutor was compelling him to absorb his words.

"My argument is as follows: Man is the product of evolution. His method of thinking, the way he uses his memory, and how he solves problems and conflicts are fixed in his DNA. *DNA is hereditary knowledge encoded in the chemical language of DNA, and reproduced in all cells of the body.* Nearly all organisms share a genetic code. Genes control such aspects as hair color, eye color and metabolism, by directing cells to make specific enzymes and other proteins.

"For an emotional species such as humans, it is believed emotion, behavior, and thoughts are passed down to the next generation and encoded in the genetic makeup. In other words, genes evolve and adapt to the particular time period. DNA is the essence of life, containing the tools of survival that is the root of the evolutionary process. This DNA, the foundation of life, was created by God, and DNA is responsible for the horrific atrocities that have occurred throughout the history of Man. Therefore, God, the Creator of DNA, is guilty of creating evil."

Prosecutor became ominously silent, his eyes penetrating Noah, seeking signs of surrender. Noah wouldn't allow it, though everything the man said—minus the God part—represented his beliefs for such a long time.

"Well," Prosecutor said, "Not bad, don't you think?"

"Not bad," Noah laughed, "but not perfect."

Prosecutor returned to his seat and folded his arms across his chest, releasing a gratified sigh. Noah sat wondering how to gather the knowledge that he acquired at school, and somehow relate it to what he had denied for so long. Observing the victorious expression on Prosecutor's face, he realized that he was going to have to, as Prosecutor said, open his mind and allow the inconceivable in.

"In order to refute your claim, I will expand on your definition of evolution."

He took a deep breath and tapped into his long-term memory.

"Evolution," Noah began, *"is large biological change that has taken place in geological history.* As you said, evolution occurs because individuals, who are genetically different, tend to leave different numbers of offspring to grow, mature, and reproduce in the following generations. As the process is repeated from generation to generation, there is a change in the genetic structure of the population.

"In Pre-Man Era, when species flourished, it was because of their basic survival instincts encoded into their DNA. I argue that the survival instinct contains the fundamental Law of Evolution commonly known as the *Food Chain*. The Food Chain is the heart of survival for all species."

"How does the Food Chain work?" Prosecutor asked.

"The pattern of the Food Chain generally says: All Food Chains begin with a *Producer*. A Producer is usually a plant, which takes in sunlight and water to make glucose as an energy source for the plant.

"Then, there is the *First Consumer*. It consumes the plant taking in the energy to perform its required functions of survival. An example of a First Consumer would be Rabbit.

"The *Second Consumer* is the third level in the Food Chain. It is the predator of the first consumer, which becomes its prey. It consumes the prey, extracting its energy from the First Consumer. For instance, Fox is a Second Consumer. Fox kills Rabbit for consumption. If Fox does not kill Rabbit, it will starve and die, unable to reproduce to the next generation. The process of evolution will be halted for Fox.

"Rabbit, a favorite prey of many carnivores, has adapted by breeding frequently and producing many young at one time, ensuring Rabbit's species does not become extinct. The Second Consumer is usually a carnivore because it cannot directly eat the plant. The Food Chain continues with its *Fourth, Fifth, Sixth Consumers*, and so on, the prey always being placed before the predator in the Food Chain.

"As the foundation of life, the Food Chain is a part of all species. It cannot be considered an evil created by God."

"This Food Chain," Prosecutor interrupted," is Man a part of it?"

"Yes, it's an unspoken and unwritten law serving as the foundation of the process of evolution. It ensures survival of the species, including Man."

"Was this law designed to include Man?"

"Yes, most definitely," Noah replied. "Man has been a tribal animal since he first walked upright. He, too, was part of the Food Chain. Because Man was bi-pedal, he could not outrun or out-climb his predators. Only in tribes could Man keep predators at a safe distance. All of Man's survival instincts were embedded into his genetic makeup long before he developed intellect. For instance, such instincts as maternal love, curiosity, and creativity are seen in most animal life.

"Over the entire four million years or more of human development, intellect developed as control over instincts to provide adaptable behavior. The more disciplined one becomes, that is, *behavior in response to intellect,* the more human he becomes. The less disciplined behavior, that is, *behavior in response to instinct,* the less human he becomes.

Once Man evolved and developed intellect and self-awareness, the basic survival instinct was transformed."

"So," Prosecutor said, "what is your fundamental argument?"

"My argument is as follows: Man transformed the basic survival instinct embedded by God to a much more self serving tool. The instinct was modified by Man to serve his own agenda, and Man violated the law by putting himself at the top of the Food Chain, leaving the other species at his mercy. Therefore, God as the catalyst of the basic instincts of survival for all species ended when Man developed intellect and self-awareness. Thus, God is not the Creator of the substance of Man, his DNA."

"Since Man is an omnivore, how did placing himself at the top of the Food Chain allow him to violate the Laws of Nature?" Prosecutor asked.

"It's not the act of placing himself at the top of the Food Chain that is the crime. It is what he did in response to being put at the top."

"What did Man do?"

"He broke the Law of Nature. For instance, in the natural world, Coyote will walk freely among a herd of antelope. The antelope will not run until Coyote pursues one of them. In accordance with the Laws of Nature, Coyote takes only what he needs to survive. Man has completely violated this law. One example is his attack on the Bison. He greedily nearly wiped these animals out of existence.

"Even today, the results of his actions are apparent. Because of global warming, the depletion of our natural resources, and the extinction of other species of animals, Man is slowly forging his way to the beginning of the extinction road. He is aware of what is happening to the planet and its species, but refuses to take any drastic measures for fear that it will cut into his profit margin.

"Man has taken complete control of the evolutionary process, and has willingly defied the fundamental Law of Nature, making Man, and Man alone, responsible for the events in human history."

In anxious silence, Noah waited for his response. Prosecutor sat with his eyes closed. Noah wished that he could read his mind, but feared what he may learn.

After a moment, Prosecutor opened his eyes and glanced at the Jury.

They nodded their heads. Prosecutor looked at Noah, revealing a softer smile. An overwhelming flood of relief engulfed Noah.

"So," Prosecutor said, "you are contending that Man is one species among millions, and his survival depended on his predecessor's instincts. Man, as an intellectual being, changed these instincts to suit his own personal needs, allowing him to take control of the evolutionary process. There is no higher spiritual force guiding the evolutionary process. It is Man, and Man alone guiding it."

"Yes," Noah replied, "that is my argument."

"Okay, if your argument is to be accepted, then it would be reasonable for Man to ask himself the following question: If those at the bottom of the Food Chain were to perish, would it mean that I too would perish?"

Prosecutor reflected for a moment, his silence pounding furiously on Noah's consciousness. He wished he had an aspirin.

"Well, an interesting argument," he said.

Feeling somewhat more brazen, Noah said thanks.

"Oh, do not thank me," he laughed. "You have only succeeded in making a small dent in my case. There are many more holes in your argument; granted, you have made enough of a case to continue with the trial, but there are still holes. Your task is to fill in each one. This will be the most difficult part of your job. Even so, I am still impressed you made it this far."

Prosecutor's eyes were heavy. Addressing the Jury, he said, "It has been an intense session. The court will take a short recess."

Before Noah could respond, a brilliant, penetrating white light engulfed him. It was so bright that he had to cover his eyes. When the light faded, he peeked through his fingers and, to his surprise, he discovered that he was no longer in the courtroom.

i.

Upon closer examination of the new surroundings, he realized that he had been brought to a playground. He didn't find Prosecutor's humor amusing.

The playground was blanketed with rich green grass, every blade groomed to exactly the same length. Scattered across the grass were several silver jungle gyms, bright red seesaws, swing sets, and slides. He felt a gentle warmth sweep across his face but could not see the sun. As he took a deep breath, the rich intoxicating air filled his lungs, and he thought that he was going to fall over. He was definitely no longer on Earth.

In the middle of the playground lay an enormous sandbox, with a small boy sitting in the middle. As he approached, he felt a knot in his stomach that twisted tighter with each step. His heart dropped suddenly—Aidan.

Aidan was wearing the same clothes that he died in, a brown T-shirt and baggy blue jeans. When he reached the sandbox, he saw that Aidan had started to build a sand castle. He looked up at him with baby blue eyes that pierced his heart. The memory of the fateful day resurfaced, watching as Aidan's limp, spiritless body toppled to the ground. An intense pain bolted through him.

Following a few seconds of aching silence, Aidan smiled. After years in hiding, innocence had finally revealed itself.

"I have been waiting a long time to see you, Noah. Come sit beside me."

Noah dutifully obeyed. The softness of the sand sedated him. He slipped his hand in it, hoping that he would not get any down his pants.

"How? I mean, why?" Noah managed to stutter.

Aidan laughed, and its sweet sound soothed Noah. He wanted to reach out and grasp him in his arms, but feared that if he did, his baby brother would vanish in a puff of smoke.

Aidan turned his attention to the sand castle. He had all of the necessary tools. Positioned against the edge of the sand box was a laundry bucket with the bottom cut out, a ruler, medium- and small-sized plant buckets, and a large pail of water. He began to pack the laundry bucket tightly with sand and water.

"Help me, Noah."

Noah again followed orders. He grabbed a bucket, knelt down beside his brother, and started to fill it, still in a state of shock.

"Noah, the Guardians have sent you to me."

"Why?"

"You are my assignment. Think of me as your own personal Guardian Angel."

"What do you mean?"

"It is my passage to becoming a *Guardian of the Light*."

"I don't understand."

"I have been watching you for a long time, Noah, and I'm not pleased with how you have evolved. It's my job to help you through the tunnel."

"Are you like a seeing-eye dog?"

"Yes, exactly," Aidan laughed. "I will guide you as best I can, but you must find the way. In order to do this, you have to look into your heart."

Aidan still looked young, but his words and the tone of his voice made him appear much older."

"Do you remember the days following my death?"

"Yes. The memories are permanently lodged within me."

"I want to talk about Dad's period of mourning."

A sharp sting slashed at Noah; he had almost forgotten that his father was dead. A nauseating feeling snuck up on him.

"After my funeral, you observed a change in Dad's behavior. He began to take Mom's religious beliefs more seriously, becoming a gentler man, more in touch with his spiritual roots. Your reaction to his change puzzles me, Noah. You were filled with bitterness and resentment toward him. Instead of participating in Mom and Dad's recovery, you withdrew.

"You were in so much pain. They could have helped you. Why didn't you reach out to them? Why were you so angry?"

Stunned at such a serious question coming from a child, Noah was speechless.

Looking down at the sand, he finally said, "When you died, Aidan, I became an atheist. It would have been pointless to reach out to them, since I did not share their beliefs."

Aidan gazed at Noah with pity in his eyes. Noah looked away. He didn't like that expression, preferring the look of admiration that he once held for him.

"Why would my death make you an atheist? That's so sad. I don't understand."

Aidan returned to smoothing out the sand blocks they had unloaded from the buckets and planters. They had dumped the planters on the larger pile of sand, revealing a three-tier base. Noah began to smooth and file the edges.

"Take your time, Noah. If we do not have a solid foundation, the castle will collapse."

Noah glanced at his brother, his face expressing that of a boy on a mission.

"You haven't answered my question."

"Well," Noah replied, "at the time, I thought that there could be no such being of goodness and light, especially one that allowed an innocent child to die, leaving a family behind to suffer the loss. I thought that if there were a God, why would he let good people die and bad people live? I came to the conclusion that since life is full of tragedy and loss, then the world could not have been created by a being of all-goodness."

"You now realize that your belief was wrong."

Noah glanced around the playground. Everything was alive, even the swing sets and slides. The tranquility consoled him.

He smiled. "Yes, apparently so. Who'da thunk it?"

Aidan giggled and said, "Many people."

"Anyway," Noah continued, "you were not there any more. The idea that you were alive in some other plane of existence was inconceivable. I thought they were wasting their lives on a fictitious being, and believed it gave them false hope. I mean, that they might see you again. There was no proof that God existed."

"There was also no proof that he didn't exist," Aidan retorted.

"True, but I believed God was a coping mechanism, an antidepressant."

Without warning, Aidan shouted, "Aha! You had certain expectations of God, and when he didn't meet your expectations, you decided that he was a myth."

"Yes, that's true."

"These expectations, where did they come from?"

" I guess from what I have heard other people say."

"Hmm, interesting."

Noah couldn't recall Aidan ever saying the phrase *Hmm, interesting.*

"So when Mom and Dad chose to believe, you shut them out."

"Yes," Noah replied.

"So you believed that your ideas were the correct ones, and Mom and Dad's were false."

"Yes."

Where is he going with this? he wondered.

"You felt that you had evolved to a higher state of awareness. Now that you were in the *know*, you decided that you no longer had a need for them. They no longer fit into your perceived world. So, in a way, you got rid of them by retreating from them."

Noah stared at him working on that stupid castle. He had a sudden urge to kick it over. He wanted to destroy it, annihilate it, but managed to restrain himself. No one had ever spoken to him that way before, especially a child. He was humiliated.

After a moment of reflecting on his words, images of instances when he withdrew to his old bedroom flashed in his mind: the neighborhood kids would come to the door and ask if he wanted to play hockey, but he always said no. He was not interested in wasting time. Noah realized where Aidan was going with this line of questioning.

What was I thinking? Why?

"Yes, Aidan, I believed that I was intellectually superior to Mom and Dad, and thought that if I shared their beliefs, I too would live in a dream world."

"Oh, I think it runs much deeper than that. You never connected, and you not only alienated yourself from Mom and Dad, you alienated yourself from life. You withdrew totally into your books and lived in isolation. In high school, you were almost always alone. You talked to people, but you never got to know anyone.

"University was the same story. Every girl that you dated eventually left once she realized she could not penetrate the shell imprisoning your being. You accomplished a lot in your young life, Noah, but at what price?"

"You don't understand," Noah said. "I wanted a life of respectability. I wanted to be recognized for my intellect. I didn't want to live a dull, ordinary life. I wanted to leave my mark on the world. I wanted to be remembered."

"You want, you want and you want," Aidan chanted.

Looking back, Noah realized he had a certain idea on how to live, and those not sharing his view became irrelevant. Loneliness started to burrow its way into his heart and for the first time in his life, he couldn't fend it off. He didn't like it.

"Gosh, Noah," Aidan laughed, "you had a huge ego."

"Yes, I guess I was full of it."

"I think full of shit is the best way to describe you." Aidan giggled.

Before he could retaliate, he was grasped by the bright light and returned to his opponent.

Round three was about to begin.

The Sinking of Noah's Ark

Chapter IV

Prosecutor rested peacefully at his table while the jury sat in calm silence.

"Hello, Noah. I hope your break was relaxing."

Detecting a trace of sarcasm, Noah stealthily replied, "No, it was not."

"I am sorry to hear that."

Noah didn't believe him. Compassion wasn't his strong suit.

Prosecutor rose from his seat, shook the creases out from his robe, and approached him.

"Now," he said, "back to business."

He said this as though he were boasting about a great victory.

"When we last left off," Prosecutor began, "you had completed your second defense, arguing that the *Food Chain* is the common thread linking all living creatures, including Man. Since the survival instinct is embedded in all living creatures, God could not have intended for the instinct to be evil, as it is a tool ensuring that evolution continues.

Prosecutor glanced at the Jury. They nodded.

"You make a good argument," he continued. "Since Man is the only species with a history of evil acts, we are forced to acknowledge that creating the basic instinct of survival was not intended to be evil. We agree with enough of your reasoning to prevent the trial from being concluded based on my previous argument concerning DNA.

"Now, I wish to explore these foundations of life further."

Noah secretly hoped that he withstood the next round better than he had his argument with Aidan. He wasn't feeling too confident.

"For my next argument," Prosecutor said, "I will bring the religion factor into the story of the evolution of Man."

Oh great, Noah thought, *this is going to be fun.*

"Once Man evolved to the point where he acquired intellect, he looked up at the stars, at the rich and diverse world laying out in perfect order for him, and had an epiphany. Man said to himself: *I do not understand how this world came to be. There must be something greater than I responsible for my existence. There must be a reason why I am here.*

"As Man looked at the other species around him, he observed the creatures surviving on their natural instincts, unable to create thought. They existed day to day, with no knowledge of space and time. Man then said to himself: *I am not like the other creatures. I have intelligence, I think, I reason, and I am inventive. I have the capability of achieving great things. Therefore, there must be a reason why I was put here to endure such hardships.*

Man then concluded: *I am superior to the other species. My life has more* meaning than theirs, so someone or something must have put me here. There must be more to life than just living, reproducing, and dying."

"Thus, came the birth of religion, or what you refer to as God, or the Gods. I will stay with the God term," he laughed. "We have to keep this as simple as possible."

Noah found that statement offensive, but said nothing. He thought that it wouldn't be wise to piss off Prosecutor.

"My argument is as follows," Prosecutor continued. "Man's awareness of God was embedded in his genetic makeup. Religion is a branch of the survival instinct. This instinct was planted by God to ensure Man had a moral code to live by. Because humans evolved to live in close proximity to one another, requiring social interaction, a moral code was essential for survival—and since religion was designed only for the intellectual species, Man, then God purposely created religion for Man. It is not part of the *Food Chain*.

"Because the horrifying acts committed by Man were carried out in the name of God, God is therefore responsible for the acts, as he is the one who implanted the instinct…and what resulted from Man's adaptation of this instinct are acts of horror and revulsion."

Prosecutor paused and grinned wickedly. Little did he realize that Noah knew exactly where he was going with this argument.

"I will now enter into evidence an example of the acts committed by Man in the name of God. The example that I will cite refers to the Spanish Inquisition that took place in medieval Europe during the fifteenth century."

He picked up a book from the table. Noah knew this was not going to be good.

"The Spanish Inquisition was carried out by Church and Government Officials for several reasons. First, *to coerce admissions of guilt from those accused of heresy or witchcraft.* Second, *to prevent free thought.* Third, *to force non-Christians into accepting Christianity as the one true faith.* And finally, *to enjoy the demented pleasure of inflicting pain.* Now, I will cite the tell-tale horrors."

Turning to a marked section, he began to read the passage slowly:

"*Foot roasting, for example, was a favorite torture method. The prisoner was immobilized, and their socks were removed to expose their bare feet. The captor smeared thick lard on the exposed flesh, then placed the feet in hot coals.*

"One other technique: *the victim was immobilized in a chair and muffled to silence his screams. An oversized copper boot was fitted over each bare foot. The torturer then slowly filled each boot with boiling oil and molten lead, peeling the flesh from the bones.*"

He paused and unveiled a slippery smile.

"The passage that I have cited is an example of Man committing bloodcurdling acts in the name of God. Man's awareness of God is a survival instinct, assigned by God to give Man a biological basis of morality. What resulted can only be described as heinous atrocities committed by Man in the name of God."

Prosecutor sighed, looking thoughtfully at Noah. "For believers in an all-good and all-knowing higher being, they certainly had a sadistic way of worshipping him."

He made a superb argument, Noah reflected. But as a man who never retreated from a challenge, he was not about to allow the trial to end this quickly.

"Yes, they did," Noah replied truthfully, "but I believe I can still disprove your argument, or at least raise some serious doubts."

Prosecutor walked to his table and sat down.

"Well," he grunted, "give it your best shot."

"The examples that you cited are indeed horrible and evil," Noah began. "They reveal the dark side of humanity. I agree with you on that point, but in order to refute your claim that God is responsible for these acts because he provided the knowledge of his existence in Man's DNA, I will have to examine the evolution of human thought."

"What do you hope to prove?"

"I hope to point out the fundamental difference between Natural Evolution and Evolution with Intent, because I believe the two exist."

"Hmm, that sounds interesting. Please continue."

Noah proceeded; although he had the feeling Prosecutor had serious doubts.

"Theories of the origin of religion have been divided into two explanations: The first, the *logical and rational*, and the second, the *psychological and irrational*. To understand how religion became a factor in human consciousness, you have to look at the biological evolution of consciousness."

Noah paused to see if Prosecutor planned on interrupting him, but he just grinned. He decided to continue before Prosecutor changed his mind.

"Amidst the murky pool of life, the first simple organisms, algae and bacteria, emerged. Their view of the world was nothing more than hazy blotches of color. When multi-cellular organisms evolved, sensing capabilities emerged; in other words, cells were able to detect light. As evolution continued, cells developed the ability to distinguish between different frequencies of light, and detect what direction the light was coming from.

"When nervous systems evolved, the primitive life forms began to process data and distribute it to other parts of the organism. As evolution continued, the increased stream of information needed an area to process all of the information.

"As brains evolved, new features were added to the consciousness. For example, the limbic system emerged in an area of the brain associated with emotion. As the brain developed, recognition and memory emerged. With primates, the larger, more elaborate brain developed, adding more properties to the consciousness. The most noteworthy property was the ability to utilize symbols. Language was beginning to appear."

Noah paused for effect. Prosecutor lifted his head and opened his mouth, but before he could speak a syllable, Noah resumed. It was a simple strategy designed to shake Prosecutor's confidence. He had no idea if it worked, since Prosecutor's face was impossible to read.

"Now," Noah continued, "it's at this significant rung in the evolutionary ladder where the natural progression of evolution takes a sharp curve and human beings evolved differently. As we grew, we were able to acquire speech. It is at this point where human evolution took on a life of its own. In other words, Man became a distinct species, detached from the evolutionary path."

Prosecutor raised an eyebrow, but Noah ignored the look and resumed.

"Being able to communicate allowed Man to share experiences with others. Man now had the ability to learn from one other, collect information, and pass it on to the next generation, leading to the groundwork of a functioning society."

Prosecutor interjected, "The primates have a functioning society."

"Yes they do, but primate societies are based on instinct. This is much different than the human species."

Suddenly, Dian Fossey stood and shouted, "I object."

She turned to walk away.

"Wait," Noah cried, "I'm not arguing that living on instinct is inferior. I'm just stating facts."

Ms. Fossey stopped, turned and looked at Prosecutor. He smiled and nodded. As she returned to her seat, relief swamped Noah.

"Being able to express thought extended Man's awareness in various ways," Noah continued. "His understanding of space expanded as he learned of events occurring outside of his immediate surroundings. Also, his comprehension of time expanded as he learned of events that had happened before his own time. Man could now reason within, and identify words with images. Thought had now formed. He could think of the future, imagining what could happen. A new inner freedom was born, the freedom to choose his own future. Free will had now come into play."

For the first time, Prosecutor revealed an important emotion: surprise. His eyes fixed on Noah's, and he was inspired.

"Thinking in words now opened the human mind to the concept of understanding. This new freedom led to Man splintering from the original evolutionary ladder. Specifically, a whole new dimension was added to human consciousness: *self-awareness*. Man could now form theories and beliefs about the world he lived in, and this new awareness led to a critical discovery: Man's own mortality. The threat of mortality brought a new and unique emotion not yet seen on the evolutionary path, the emotion known as *irrational fear*."

Prosecutor interrupted, "Irrational fear?"

"Yes. Irrational fear didn't exist on the evolutionary path before, because it served no purpose, and it still doesn't. This fear only deteriorated thought processes, and it was Man's response to this fear that led to the discovery of God. Irrational fear is unique to Man, and remarkably different from fear in the animal world."

"How so?" Prosecutor asked.

"For instance, the *fight or flight* response associated with the animal world. This instinct ensures a chance of survival. An animal such as Mouse, when perceiving danger, will not sit there and rationalize how to deal with the threat.

"When presented with danger, the sudden surge of adrenalin provokes Mouse to run. It is a spur-of-the-moment reaction."

"The reaction can be paralleled to that of a person about to be run over by a car," Prosecutor interjected. "He does not think about what action to take. He automatically jumps out of the way. This is a survival instinct encoded into your DNA."

"Yes, it is much different from the emotion of irrational fear. The fundamental difference between the two is this: Irrational fear is brought about by reasoning, and how Man chose to pacify this fear was self-created, a decision of his own making. I argue that religion did evolve from the survival instinct, but it was Man who created, interpreted and exploited it to the *psychologically irrational*."

Prosecutor and the Jury were looking at Noah with apprehension.

"Are you saying that Man's awareness of a higher power evolved out of a senseless emotion?"

"No, of course not," Noah laughed, "that wouldn't make any sense. I'm saying that Man's perception of God is a product of irrational fear. I argue that the initial awareness of spirituality and higher goodness was intended to be used as a tool for survival."

"You will have to show why you think religion was designed to be a survival tool." Prosecutor said.

"I believe I can justify my argument by addressing the origins of primitive religion."

"Very well, please proceed."

Noah does so under a cloud of doubt.

"Primitive religion originated as a collection of social structures and rituals that allowed the individual to function within the society. Myths enabled religious symbols to be put into story form, and they not only provided an overall view of the world, but also the instruments to figure it out. For example, almost all primitive religions believed puberty and marriage symbolized children acquiring adult roles in the community and culture. Most primitive religions consider the events to be meaningful to the society and culture. Rituals are also associated with the beginning of a new year, and with planting and harvesting times. In hunting and gathering societies, rituals are supposed to increase game and give the hunter greater strength."

"So," Prosecutor interrupted, "rituals performed during occasional events such as droughts and other natural disasters are usually intended to pacify higher powers who might be the cause."

"Yes, therefore, I argue that the religious instinct embedded in Man was implanted by God to be used as an instrument of human survival, and to generate his awareness to Man. The purpose: To help Man understand his world with the limited knowledge he had, and to instill the concept of goodness and compassion. Because of that reason, the religious instinct cannot be viewed as evil."

"So what separates harmless worship of the primitive cultures from that of the Spanish Inquisition?" Prosecutor asked.

"The atrocities that you cited are not the result of the natural instinct embedded in our genetic makeup. It is not an instinct at all. It is the result of the evolution of free will. You see, the ability to determine true morality emerged with intellect. The awareness of a higher being evolved when Man became an intelligent and freethinking species, and with that development came the ability to choose compassion, to believe in higher goodness, and to believe superiority is a false ideal. The knowledge of the Creator, and the knowledge of true morality, was embedded within Man. As an intellectual being, Man was given the choice of how to follow the ideals. He had the ability to choose goodness. God gave that to Man through free will.

"In essence, free will was designed to ensure independence, and the freedom to grow both spiritually and intellectually."

"So Man just decided out of the blue to start torturing people," Prosecutor snarled.

"No, of course not. It runs much deeper than that."

"I should hope so. For a second, I thought that you were going to enter a plea of insanity."

Noah started to laugh and said, "That would be an interesting argument, but I don't think I will go down that road."

"That is a good decision," Prosecutor chuckled. "You would definitely lose."

"Yes, I agree, but in order to explain how one evolves from performing harmless rituals to committing acts of hate, I will have to return to an important issue that you raised in your argument."

"And that issue would be?"

"You said that as Man developed intellect and self-awareness, he looked up into the sky and realized the vastness of the world he resided in. When he looked at the other species around him, he realized he was different, above living on survival instincts alone. Therefore, someone greater must be responsible for his existence."

"Yes, that was my testimony."

"In fact," Noah continued, "Man determined that he was superior to all the other species, so there must be a reason why he was put on earth. Then Man's awareness of God emerged. The awareness of God evolved out of the survival instinct, but the catalyst was not the result of God's intervention. There is one crucial step you failed to mention in your argument. This step occurred when Man's awareness of God evolved out of an irrational fear of his own mortality, and discovering he was not like the other species inhabiting the world. These two circumstances led to the emergence of a further critical emotion—*arrogance*. I argue that arrogance is a crucial component of the evolution of Man."

At this point, Noah realized that he needed to demonstrate how this happened. He looked around the room and observed a collection of papers lying on Prosecutor's table.

"If I could have a sheet of paper and a pen," he said, "I would like to illustrate the process in a chart."

Without responding, Prosecutor walked over to the table, picked up the paper and pen, and delivered it to Noah.

Placing the paper on his lap, he said, "Here is how it started,"

Survival Instinct → Intellect → Free Will → Irrational Fear → Arrogance Self-Aware

Handing the paper to Prosecutor to analyze and pass on to the Jury, he resumed his testimony.

"Initially, the awareness of a higher being served as a foundation of morality. Man no longer functioned on his natural instincts. He was evolving intellectually, and as a freethinking species, Man had the ability to conceive his own morality. The atrocities that you cited cannot be contributed to God, because the awareness of a higher power was not designed to be evil. It was Man himself who adopted arrogance, and it was his arrogance that formed his moral basis. He did this with the knowledge of a higher power of all-goodness.

"By his own free will, Man created a groundwork of ethics and morality rooted in arrogance."

"So," Prosecutor intervened, "once Man developed intellect, the ability to reason, and free will, he became evolved enough to know the difference between right and wrong, and good and evil."

"Yes, but unfortunately arrogance led Man down a different path. Since Man took this path by choice, God can't be found guilty of instilling his presence in order to create evil. Through Man's earliest flaw, his adoption of arrogance, he alone created morality, not God. I argue that arrogance is a human creation, not a Godly one."

Noah paused, taking a deep breath. He was impressed with his logic. He was not sure by the puzzled expression on Prosecutor's face, but he thought that he might have given him something to think about.

"Okay," Prosecutor said, "based on your argument, Man could ask himself the following question: Since I think, therefore I know that I am. So, if what I think is terribly flawed, then what am I?"

"Yes, exactly."

"An interesting argument," he said, "but there is much more to it than just saying arrogance is responsible for the evil acts that I provided in my argument. You cannot suddenly veer from arrogance to torture. It is not that simple."

"No, it is not, I realize that there is a large gap between arrogance and evil that has to be filled in. I am arguing that the initial intent of instilling the awareness of God cannot be considered a catalyst of evil. If you can accept my argument on the condition that I can fill in the gap, I believe I can do so."

Prosecutor reflected for a moment while at the same time Noah wondered if he could or if, as Aidan would say, he was full of shit.

"Yes, I can do that," Prosecutor said, "but not now. The Jury and I require another recess to examine the testimony you have given thus far."

Before Noah could utter a syllable, the light pounced on him.

ii.

Noah opened his eyes to find himself back in the playground with Aidan. The rich green trees replenished his spirit. The blue jays and sparrows flying above him seemed to emanate joy.

As he walked to the sand box, he discovered that during his absence, his brother had been busy. He had completed the three-tier base and professionally smoothed it to perfection.

When Noah approached, he noticed that Aidan had added three towers to each corner, and was currently working on the fourth. He was in the process of taking small mounds of sand mixed with water and rubbing them between his hands. As Noah sat next to him, he began to form a peak-like structure to the tower that thinned out as he moved his hands toward the top of the pile. Noah began to do the same.

"You have accomplished a lot since we last talked." Noah said.

"I could say the same about you," he replied coolly.

Aidan automatically picked up where they last left off. There was no *hello, how are you?* Noah was hurt.

"I concluded our last conversation by saying that you were full of shit."

"Yes you did," he laughed, "but I have since discovered a more appropriate word to describe me."

"What word would that be?"

Noah could tell by the tone in Aidan's voice that he knew exactly what he was going to say.

"Arrogant."

"Ah, arrogant," Aidan giggled, "a good description. But now I want to focus on your life at Walden's Cove."

Noah knew they were going to go down that road.

"Growing up at the Cove, you always felt you did not belong. Why?"

Noah knew that question was going to surface.

"Do you remember Mr. Weatherfield's Variety Store?" Noah asked.

"Yes."

"Every time we went into the store, do you remember what Mr. Weatherfield would say after we paid?"

"Yes," Aidan laughed. "He would say, 'See ya later, alligators,' and we would say, 'In a while, crocodile.'"

"That was how I regarded Walden's Cove," Noah said. "Every day people would get up, go to work, come home, eat dinner, watch television and then go to bed. Their lives were like a needle skipping on a record player, the same part of the song constantly repeated. That was how I saw daily life in the community, a constant repetition of the day before, stuck in a state of repetitiveness.

"How well did you know Mr. Weatherfield?" Aidan asked.

Noah reflected on Mr. Weatherfield's warm smile and the eyes that danced with delight every time Aidan charged through the door.

"Not well, just enough to chat with when I went into the store."

"Then I guess you didn't know that he was a poet."

"What?" Noah blurted out.

"Yes, a poet. On many early weekend mornings, while you were sleeping, he would pack a lunch, and with his pen and notepad in hand, he would hike to an isolated area by the shore. He sat on the rocks and captured every second of the sunrise. It was during this time that he would write wonderful prose."

"Wow," Noah said. "I didn't know."

Noah tried to envision Mr. Weatherfield, with his shaggy gray beard, plaid shirt and blue suspenders, sitting by the shore in a state of inspiration.

They had finished constructing the towers. Aidan started to dig out the center for a courtyard. Noah joined him. In spite of his interrogation and personal attacks, Noah was enjoying himself, and wished their time together would last an eternity. He had deeply missed his brother, and to have this second chance was incredible. He wanted to remember every second.

"If you would like," Aidan continued, "I could recite a list of many other residents with similar stories."

"No, that's not necessary, I get your point. You see, I wanted my life to be meaningful, and I wanted to evolve intellectually. To do this, I felt I had to break all ties with the community."

"And this included Mom and Dad?"

"Yes, Mom and Dad too. To me, they were a part of a nowhere community, and I believed that in order to achieve my goals, I had to break my link with them."

"And now Dad is dead, and you never got to know the man who could have taught you so much. You denied him."

" I know," Noah sighed. "I was wrong. As I said, I was arrogant. I had this idea of how I wanted to live and abandoned those who were so much a part of me. It was pure arrogance."

"Oh, it was more than arrogance. You were selfish."

Noah reflected on Aidan's stinging words. Images of the past flashed through his mind—his father gently tapping on his bedroom door, asking him if he wanted to help him down at the wharf. Noah's reply: "Maybe next time."

"Yes," Noah said, "I guess I was selfish."

"And your selfishness cost you love, family and happiness."

"Yes, it did."

Noah was feeling like a big schmuck. All of his life, he looked at the town as a whole, never taking the time to look at the parts that made it. He wondered what his life would have been like if he had.

"The search you undertook to prove that God was a myth cost you so much," Aidan said. "It could be argued that by seeking to destroy God, you in fact destroyed yourself."

Noah was humiliated. Aidan knew so much about him.

"Before you are summoned to court, I want you to think about something."

"Okay," Noah mumbled.

He had already given him enough to think about.

"This God that people have used to justify their evil acts, is this the same God you are now defending?"

Before Noah could respond, the white light approached, and returned him to the courtroom.

The Sinking of Noah's Ark

Chapter V

eated at the table, an unusual expression was displayed on Prosecutor's face. His smile was that of a docile man, and his eyes were not as dim.

The jury appeared the same. Noah was starting to wonder if they were mannequins.

About five feet to Noah's right, he noticed a new addition to the room: a blackboard with a plentiful supply of white chalk. When Prosecutor saw him staring at it, he laughed and said, "No one can say I neglect the needs of my witness."

"Yeah," Noah indulged him, "you are a swell guy."

Prosecutor snickered, "Well, Noah, I hope you had a much more enjoyable break?"

"I wouldn't say enjoyable," Noah replied. "More like...productive."

"Good. Are you ready to begin?"

"I'm as ready as I will ever be."

Prosecutor rose from his desk and approached. He was not as intimidating, his jaw more relaxed. Noah allowed his own muscles to slacken.

"During your previous testimony," Prosecutor said, "you argued that it was Man's arrogance that is responsible for the evil acts committed throughout human history. I had pointed out that there is a large gap between arrogance and evil. For instance, an arrogant person does not necessarily go out and commit evil acts."

He paused and sighed deeply.

"So, we will now be heading down a dark and gloomy terrain lying within Man's consciousness."

He lowered his eyes, deepened his voice and said, "The nature of evil."

The comfort Noah had felt was slipping away.

"After careful examination of your testimony," Prosecutor began, "I'm able to make a further argument. I agree when you say that Man is different from animals because he is the only species who commits horrifying acts of evil. This means that Man is terribly flawed. Although God did not directly create Man, he is part of the evolutionary process, as it was God who initiated the Big Bang. Since Man is flawed, this makes God guilty of initiating a sequence of events resulting in the creation of a flawed species. The clincher of my argument is as follows: God embedded the knowledge of himself in Man, and Man chose to justify his evil acts in the name of God.

"One would think that Man, having the knowledge of an all-good and powerful being, would have chosen an alternate path, but he did not. The history of Man has been about the evolution of the mind. As Man became more intelligent, he should have learned from his mistakes and realized the atrocities that he committed in the past were immoral. Upon this discovery, he would try to change his beliefs and become a more moral species, but he has not done this because human history is riddled with one atrocity after another."

Prosecutor paused and walked over to his table. He picked up a new book and turned to a marked passage.

Uh-oh, Noah thought, *here comes another one.*

"I will now enter into evidence an example of the results of Man's chosen path. I submit the passage because it is a written historical account, witnessed firsthand and recorded in a diary. It reveals the essence of Man's beliefs in God."

Prosecutor grinned evilly. "The passage was written by a man known as Bartolome De Las Casas. Bartolome De Las Casas was a Spaniard ordained into the Priesthood in 1511. He recorded the atrocities committed by the Spanish Christians toward the native peoples residing in Cuba and on the Island of Hispaniola."

Prosecutor cleared his throat, threw a quick glare at Noah and said, "I will now read excerpts from Bartolome's journal:

Of the Spaniards who called themselves Christians, on the Island of Hispaniola was where they first perpetrated their ravages and oppressions on the native peoples. The most powerful ruler of the islands had to see his own wife raped by a Christian officer. They took infants from their mother's breast, snatching them by the legs and pitching them headfirst against the crags or grasping them by the arms and throwing them into the rivers, roaring with laughter and saying " boil there, you offspring of the devil."

Among the noteworthy outrages they committed was the one perpetrated against a Cacique, a very important noble, by the name of Hatuey. When tied to the stake, the Cacique Hatuey was told by a Franciscan Friar who was present, an artless rascal, something about the God of the Christians and of the faith. He was told what he could do in the brief time that remained to him in order to be saved and go to heaven. The Cacique, who had never heard of any of this, was told he would go to the Inferno if he did not adopt Christian faith, and would suffer eternal torment. He asked the Franciscan Friar if Christians all went to heaven.

When told that they did, he said he would prefer to go to hell.

Hatuey was then burned alive.

Prosecutor fell silent, allowing the events he had cited to settle in. He walked over to his table and seated himself.

"I submit this passage," he said, "as an example of how Man has honored God. Throughout human history, the concept of God has always remained with Man. In spite of this knowledge, Man has continually wreaked havoc on all species, including his own. This tragically flawed species doesn't have the ability to evolve to a higher moral plane of existence, and therefore must be eliminated."

Prosecutor did not reveal a triumphant look this time, only a disgusted expression. Feeling disgusted as well, Noah reluctantly proceeded.

"You have made an argument that can be considered a sweeping generalization. As you said earlier, I have to fill in the holes, and by doing so, I will disprove your argument."

Prosecutor leaned his head back and stared at the ceiling.

"I believe this is going to take a while," he murmured.

After hearing the previous passage, Noah had to agree.

"How Man arrived at the point where he could commit the horrible acts that you cited is the core of my defense," Noah began. "I will now return to the point in human history where Man, out of his own arrogance, created a flawed foundation of morality. It's at this point where Man developed his superiority complex and simultaneously became aware of God. It is my intention to prove that Man did not become aware of the Creator. It was through his own arrogance that Man believed he was created in an image of God.

"My argument is as follows: Man created God in an image of himself. At the moment where he created God in arrogance, he actually created a being that would serve his own agenda. What cultivated from this was Man's self-created foundation of morality, not the Creator's. What propagated from this genetically modified seed was a network of prejudice, oppression, hate, and evil."

"Wait," Prosecutor interrupted. "I want to make sure I understand your position. You are saying that Man's awareness of God is actually a myth employed to justify his cruel acts, and to maintain control over his own species and environment. This myth has evolved throughout generations, so it is actually embedded in his genetic makeup, evolving each generation to suit the needs of Man."

"Yes."

Noah's reluctance had now faded.

"You see," Noah continued, "Man was blessed with intellect. With intellect comes reasoning, and with reasoning comes choice. Man opted for the choice better suited to his needs—arrogance. The choice was made a long time ago, and as Man evolved, so did his arrogance. What sprouted from this seed was the unfolding of human oppression. As human morality evolved, it embedded itself in man's DNA. It became a reality."

"Give me an example," Prosecutor barked.

Noah thought for a moment while Prosecutor tapped his foot. The echo was maddening.

"Okay," Noah said. "I will give an example of one of the most notorious figures in human history—Adolph Hitler."

Prosecutor nodded his head, as if he knew that name was going to emerge.

"Hitler believed that he was the chosen one and under divine protection. Hitler's supporters made great effort in promoting the belief that he was perfect. When he fulfilled his promises, people started seeing Hitler as no longer a man, but as a Messiah. Public meetings exhibited a religious atmosphere, with stages designed to create a supernatural experience. When

Hitler appeared onstage, it was more becoming of a God than a Man."

"Why have you given this example?" Prosecutor shouted. "What is the point?"

"I have cited this example because it can be considered the development of a dark and evil cult. Successful religions typically begin as cults, and then increase in power once they achieve acceptance outside of their initial membership. Their power grows if they can persuasively claim the leaders have special access to God. Once they achieve power, they have complete control and can justify all of their acts in the name of God."

"So," Prosecutor interrupted, "once the cult evolves into religion, what is at the center of this new religion?"

"At the center of each religion lies an explanation of how the world began, and how its members arrived at its core. The devotees of each religion compete as a tribe with those of other religions, with the beliefs becoming ingrained in the human psyche."

"Now that Man possessed this comprehension of life," Prosecutor interrupted, "he could now control it. It gave him power, feeding his hunger for control over all others."

"Yes, Man's religious drive is based on far more than spirituality and establishing moral values. His conscious mind greedily sought an eternal afterlife. Religion itself evolved from a bed of ethics, and it has likely always been used in one manner or another to justify moral codes."

"So," Prosecutor interjected, "you are arguing that the people of Germany were emotionally driven to believe in someone promising to restore their country. When Hitler did this, they willingly put him on a pedestal. Hitler and his men were then able to control and brainwash the masses into believing that he was their savior."

"Yes. The Nazis knew exactly how to exploit human weakness. You see, with the power to create rises the power to generate illusions. Depending on the circumstance, the illusion, whether good or evil, will be readily adopted. What happened in Nazi Germany was not based on any instinct instilled in human DNA. It is an example of how Man altered his DNA to serve his own selfish desires. It was a method implemented by a deranged desire to rule the world."

Pausing for a moment, Noah observed Prosecutor leaning forward, arms stretched outward on his table, and eyes fixed on the bare wall behind the empty Judge's seat. The deadly silence crept up on Noah.

"If you will," Noah cracked, "I would like to demonstrate how the evolution of man unfolded. I will begin my chart at arrogance."

With a quick wave of the hand, Prosecutor motioned Noah to the blackboard. Noah slipped out of his seat, walked over, picked up a piece of chalk, and began illustrating:

Free Will → Irrogance → God → Morality → Selfish Gene

Lie

After completing the diagram, he returned to his seat, deciding to give Prosecutor and the Jury a moment to study his work before resuming his testimony.

Noah studied each juror. A few scratched their heads with confused frowns while others revealed understanding grins.

"My argument is as follows: Man's arrogance led to the creation of his concept of God, which led to Man interpreting his own set of morality and ethics. How he interpreted morality was at the core of the evolution of the human mind. Because Man's interpretation of morality was self-serving, it inevitably led to the encoding of the *selfish gene* as part of his genetic make up, and how the *selfish gene* became encoded and perpetuated was the result of Man's implementation of intellect and free will to human behavior."

"That sounds good in theory," Prosecutor said, "but we need facts."

"Okay, I can give you facts. For example, all of the higher animals use past experience as an important part of their behavioral decisions. As with many other species, *the behavior of humans is determined by how they perceive past experience. Past experience includes: training, education and environmental influences.*

As evolution continued, the *selfish gene* became modified by influences on mental development. The changes are passed down by Man from generation to generation, and altered to fit his self-serving ideals of the particular time period. Man, not God, implemented these changes because Man is an intellectual species with free will. God did not implant the selfish gene, it was created and implanted by Man. As the evolutionary process continued, the gene became the catalyst of further modifications in his DNA. Therefore, God cannot be held responsible for creating the selfish gene, because Man is."

Prosecutor revealed a pleasantly perplexed smile. Noah hoped that he was starting to respect his intelligence.

"Are you saying that organized religion and the Creator of the universe are two completely different entities?"

"Yes," Noah replied. "Religion was created by a small group of selfish individuals to replace the true nature of the Creator. The creation of organized religion was designed to ensure the survival of a self-chosen few, not all."

Noah's confidence was radiating. He tried to contain it, but Prosecutor smirked.

"From what you have just argued," Prosecutor said, "Man could ask himself the following question: If I am to believe that I am the chosen one, then what does it mean if my belief actually makes me the unchosen?"

Prosecutor closed his eyes. Noah didn't think he should respond. After a moment Prosecutor opened his eyes and smiled.

"Well Noah, that's not bad, not bad at all. I'm not sure about this so-called *selfish gene,* and how it evolved to result in such horrific atrocities, but your argument is sound enough to prevent me from concluding the trial thus far. Even so, I need more explanations."

"And I'm prepared to provide them."

"Okay," he said, "but I require another recess. The jury requires time to absorb your testimony."

On that note, the white light approached and returned Noah to his brother.

iii.

Aidan had a beautiful piece of artwork sitting before him. During Noah's absence, he completed the courtyard and constructed several magnificent arches. He was now adding intricately detailed features to each arch. As Noah sat next to him, he was carving cathedral windows with a pallet knife. Aidan passed Noah a knife that was lying beside him.

Without interrupting his work, Aidan began to speak.

"This is a beautiful place."

Noah scanned the playground; the grass and sky were alluring. He wanted to stretch out on the grass and sleep for a while.

"Yes, it's remarkable."

"Unbelievable would be a more appropriate word," Aidan giggled.

"Yes," Noah laughed, "unbelievable."

"Now that you have faced this trial," Aidan continued, "you've come to realize that there is a higher power, and knowing this, you have to accept not only his presence, but his presence along with my untimely death."

Aidan glanced up at him, revealing a mischievous smile.

"Are you angry with God? Can you live in a world where good people die while evil people live content lives?"

"Yes, Noah sighed. "It's a painful acceptance, but I believe that I can."

"Tell me how you can accept this reality."

"Well, now when I reflect on your death, I can look at it differently. Although your death was senseless and unfair, I realize that it was an unfortunate accident. I mean, it was a mistake. You were so young. You forgot the helmet, and the other driver couldn't see you. If he had, he would have stopped."

"That's right, a person can't control everything. Death is as real as life and you can't escape it. Our fate is the same as any other species. We try hard to cheat death, but in the end we are all faced with the knowledge of our own mortality."

"Unfortunately," Noah said, "events sometimes occur which shorten our lives, but that's life, unpredictable and out of our control. I believe that we are special to God, but I suppose all creatures are special to him. If he preferred one species to another, he would be prejudiced, and that would be illogical since a being of all-goodness cannot be prejudiced. I guess that it was humans, not the Creator, who decided that they were the superior species."

"It could explain all of the terrible things humans do to one another in the name of superiority."

Aidan face turned a deep shade of red. Noah thought that he was going to cry.

"Yes," Noah said, "I guess it could."

"It makes me sad, Noah, very sad."

"Me too."

"So, you don't blame God for my death?"

"No, I don't. It wasn't his fault. It was nobody's fault. It was just a terrible accident."

"Are you at peace with it?"

"Yes, I'm at peace with it."

Aidan stopped carving, looked up at Noah and smiled innocently. Noah started to weep. With no one to blame, and no one to be angry with, all he felt was sadness. Noah was in mourning. He was looking into his brother's eyes and mourning his death.

"Ten years is a long time to carry the pain with you, Noah."

"Yes, it is."

Aidan began to laugh and said, "But what can you do? You are only human."

Noah started to laugh through the tears, but was interrupted by the light.

Chapter VI

"Welcome back, Noah."

Prosecutor and the Jury were waiting for him. Noah wiped his eyes dry and shook off his emotions.

Prosecutor's eyes had undergone further changes. Looking into them, Noah noticed a glimmer of light. When he saw it, he felt something foreign to him—hope. Perhaps his testimony was making an impact. He was not sure.

Prosecutor remained seated and picked up where they previously left off.

"When we finished our last discussion, you had argued that it was Man's arrogance that led to the development of the selfish gene. I do not understand how a selfish person could perform the atrocities that have taken place throughout human history."

"A selfish person would not," Noah said, "but the way this gene evolved led to such acts. I would like to explain."

"Very well."

"Do you remember that I previously said theories of the evolvement of religion were divided into two positions—one, *intellectual and rational*, and the other, *psychological and irrational*?"

"Yes, I remember."

"I will now explain what I meant."

He paused and took a deep breath. Aidan was still with him.

I have to focus, he whispered.

"It is my argument that religion evolved from these two conditions creating a division and modification of the selfish gene. Richard Dawkins first proposed the selfish gene. He believed that a gene is selfish if it forces its host to spread the selfish pattern of behavior or thought. He suggests that evolution takes place entirely through the effects of natural selection on the development of the genes. *Genes are selfish, not altruistic.*

"Dawkins poses that the struggle for survival always takes place at the individual gene. A concept or idea survives if individuals pass it on either to each other, or to the next generation. Like the common cold, for example: when one sneezes, he passes it to another, who in turn passes it to another.

"According to Dawkins, *God indeed exists, if only as a pattern in the brain structures replicated across the minds of billions of people throughout the world.*

"So, evolution occurs because different individuals, who are genetically different, tend to leave different numbers of offspring to grow, mature, and reproduce in the following generation. As this process is repeated from generation to generation, there is a change in the genetic structure of the population. When the selfish gene is passed on, it alters thought patterns, and in turn behavior patterns, causing the gene to propagate the pattern."

"Okay," Prosecutor interjected, "if a selfish gene is put forth into a population, the selfish individual benefits, but the others helping him do not benefit because the selfish person does not return the favor."

"That's correct; the selfish individual is better off than the selfless individual. Dawkins believes that in time, selfless individuals adopt the selfish individual's pattern of behavior. Therefore, selfishness infects others, replicates, and is passed down to the next generation. It is this pattern of behavior perpetuating the evolutionary passage of the selfish gene."

"Are you saying Man's behavior and morality are determined by his genes?" Prosecutor asked.

"No," Noah firmly replied, "it's the other way around. It is at this point I argue that the animal behavior patterns allowing the passage of their survival instincts separates from the human genetic evolution of the selfish gene."

"How so?"

"Behaviorism as applied to animals is a natural phenomenon. This means the material world is the ultimate reality, and everything can be explained in natural laws. Man is different, as he is more than just a machine responding to conditioning. You cannot predict or control human behavior, nor shape morality by controlling rewards and punishments. The ethical consequences of applying behaviorism to humans are that it exonerates Man from his moral responsibilities. I argue that it is behavior, combined with intellect and free will, determining the evolutionary passage of the selfish gene."

"How does the selfish gene evolve?"

"Because of human intellect and free will, I argue that it evolves into two separate genes: The propensity to believe and adopt the Lie, known as the *self-deception gene*, and the propensity to believe and adopt the truth, known as the *self-realization gene*. I will first discuss the Lie, because it is embracing the self-deception gene which has led to the embracement of evil."

This time Noah did not wait for permission to approach the blackboard. He stood facing the blackboard, feeling the Jury's eyes boring into the back of his head. He would have to be creative. He picked up the chalk with his quivering hand:

The Story of The Phibs and The Aphibs

Free Will → Arrogance → God → Morality
Selfish Gene
Aphibs ←   *→Phibs*

Truth   *Lie*

Self-Realization Gene   *Self-Deception Gene*

Returning to his seat, Noah observed Prosecutor crinkle his nose, eyes closed to a squint. He continued under Prosecutor's and the Jury's suspect eyes.

"My argument is as follows: The self-deception gene evolved from the point where Man first decided he was superior to all other species. To justify his views, Man created a God to mirror his beliefs, and his God served his own selfish desires, leading to the development of his own set of moral values and ethics. Man selfishly created a myth about God that inevitably led to instituting lies to justify his convictions. The lies served as physical justification for the beliefs. Thus, the birth of the Phibs."

"Aha," Prosecutor laughed. "Tell me more about the myths."

"The myths provided the tools for deciphering the world as the Phibs saw it. The religious symbols allowed believers to be in touch with this God. The believers lived according to how a small group of Phibs decided they should live."

Without warning, John Humphrey stood and said, "I object."

He turned from Noah and began to walk away.

"Wait," Noah cried, "please let me explain."

He stopped and turned around. Sighing, he returned to his seat.

"Thank you," Noah said.

He conveyed nothing.

"The Jury aren't fools," Prosecutor said. "Be warned."

"Okay," Noah muttered.

"Now," Prosecutor said, "how did the Phibs persuade the masses to adopt their value system?"

"How they did this was absolute genius," Noah replied. "I will explain: In Europe before the eighteenth century, governments were under the direction of the Church. Many controversies, quarrels, and wars resulted.

"The priests, who were delegates of the communities, presented government officials with instructions and regulations that were made into laws. The laws were designed to supervise the behavior of the people. Disobeying the laws was considered resistance to government and Church, and those breaking the laws were severely punished.

"The main function of the government was to protect the Church and enforce its ideals. So, how Phib perceived his God inevitably set the stage for the evolution of thought."

Noah paused to get a second wind, wishing he had a glass of water.

"My argument is as follows: The Phibs created their God as a means of maintaining control over an increasing and diverse human population. The horrors that you described were not committed in the name of the Creator, but in the name of the Phibs' God. Therefore, since the Phibs created God in an image of themselves, they committed the crimes in the name of Man. When Phib altered his genes, he dismissed the idea of an all-knowing, all-good, and all-powerful being because it did not fit into his own selfish agenda."

"That sounds good in theory," Prosecutor said, "but I need evidence."

"Okay, I will give you an example. When the Christian Spaniards came across the native peoples of the New World, they saw that the people were different. They dressed differently, had a different skin color, and their culture and spiritual beliefs were different.

"When the Spaniards saw all of the natural resources that could be harvested from this new world, they salivated greedily. They saw the different people as obstacles to the riches, and their differences were then viewed as deviant.

"Phib's greed turned to hate. He said to himself: *These primitive, godless savages don't deserve to have all of these riches. These people are inferior.*"

This time it was Sitting Bull who rose from his seat and yelled, "I object."

He had a disgusted look on his face.

"Please, sir," Prosecutor said. "I believe the man is going to make a point."

Sitting Bull grunted and sat down.

"So what did Phib do?" Prosecutor asked.

"Phib set out to eradicate the native people, inflicted the most evil atrocities upon them. Because of greed, hate, and the belief that native people were inferior and godless, Phib set out to destroy them. To the Christians, native people were no better than animals.

"To justify their actions, the Phibs had the written word as moral justification, one with commandments and self-serving political motives."

"What do you mean by the written word?"

"The Bible, for instance, was not delivered to Man by God. It was elected as the word of God by a group of men in the fourth century. During this time, Christian leaders could not agree which books would be the word of God, so the Roman Emperor at that time, Emperor Constantine, offered church leaders money to agree on a book that could be used by all Christians as the Word of God. The Church leaders assembled and voted Man's God into existence. Even back then, money was the almighty power."

"And the Bible can be shown to be not the true word of the Creator?"

"Oh, yes. When reading the Bible, one can conclude the book is not the word of the Creator, as there are factual errors clearly written in it. For example, the Bible says that the world is flat, which conflicts with what we now know. The Bible declares the earth does not move, where we now know as a fact that the earth does move. And, according to the Bible, *the cause of mental illness is demonic possession*, but today we know this isn't true. It is also said a star moved across the sky until it was directly over the town of Bethlehem, but science now proves this cannot happen.

"It would have been great if the Bible had spoken against bigotry, and prohibited slavery and the oppression of women, but it did not. It condones slavery and contains rules discriminating against women. Also, God apparently killed people, and ordered people to be killed.

"I argue that the Bible is physical evidence confirming Phib created his God, not the other way around, and these guidelines written by Phib served to justify his actions."

Prosecutor eyed the Jury and chuckled, "At least he has read the book."
The Jury smirked.

"What proof do you have to support your argument?" Prosecutor continued.

"That is simple," Noah replied. "For example, ethnic hatred was common throughout human history. Jews have been historically persecuted. In medieval times, they were blamed for the plague and depicted as having horns and cloven feet, as well as sacrificing Christian babies. Also, during the Crusades, Jews were murdered by Christians."

Noah glanced over at Albert Einstein to see his eyes glass over. He did not like bringing up horrible memories for a man that he had so much respect for, but unfortunately he could not avoid it, since he had to concentrate on his case.

"Jews were often the victims of bigotry, boycotts, exclusions, restrictive laws, assaults, and murder long before the Holocaust." Noah continued.

"Are you saying that the Bible is evil?" Prosecutor asked.

An image of his mother suddenly flashed in Noah's mind.

"Oh no, the Bible has spiritual information in it, but there are a few statements that can be considered self-serving. I think it is important to be aware of these statements before one embraces the Bible in its entirety. The Bible was written a long time ago; therefore, it is important to realize that there is information in it that does not apply to today's society. It is how Man adopts the information and incorporates it into daily life that influences his pattern of thinking. The Bible can only be used to spread evil if one chooses it for that purpose.

"In other words, how one interprets God determines how one interprets the Bible."

The Jury nodded and smiled. Noah was exhilarated.

"Basically," Prosecutor said, "Man should ask himself: If the Bible disappeared, does that mean God would also disappear?"

At this point, Noah felt that it would be appropriate to extend his diagram to illustrate the next step in the evolution of the human mind. He rose and proceeded to the blackboard:

→ *Phib*

Free Will →Lie →Self-Deception Gene →Hate →Evil Gene

Noah returned to his seat and continued his testimony.

"I contend that the Creator could not have implanted the self-deception gene. Man created this gene. Evolution of the human mind was not pre-set. It was based on choice, Man's choice, and the results of his choice are a burden for Man to bear.

"When humans evolved, they developed intellect and the ability to reason. They began to make choices, and these choices influenced their behavior, which in turn dictated how their genetic makeup would evolve."

"So" Prosecutor said, "you are arguing that intellect and the ability to learn are the building blocks of the evolution of the selfish gene. How one perceives life, himself, and others are the determining components of evolution, which in turn determines Man's morality."

"Yes. For generations, humans have been searching for reasons to justify their beliefs and actions. Blaming it on our genetic makeup is just another way of not facing the truth about our past. My argument: We are flawed by choice, and our history has unfolded because of our own arrogant choices.

"Arrogance is not the result of the Creator. Arrogance is the result of human intellect and free will.

"The fundamental flaw in human nature is the inability to accept the blame. By not accepting responsibility, we have never been able to achieve higher consciousness. In essence, we are the product of the Lie.

"Why can't humans see that their truth is a lie?"

"The Lie is so much a part of us," Noah replied, "and so much effort has been exerted to maintain it, if we accept that the truth is a lie, then we have to accept our existence is based on a lie. We would then be forced to realize that the horrific events in history could have been avoided. That is the number one fact we cannot accept, because if we accept it, then we have to accept we are not the morally superior species we thought we were."

Noah had to pause for a moment. He could feel his heart pounding. He was so full of anger and pain, so full of guilt. His tirade would not help his case.

"Noah, slow down," Prosecutor laughed. "Why are you in such a hurry to explain? By now, I thought that you would have realized that the passage of time is irrelevant here. How slow or fast you give your testimony has little effect on the verdict."

He didn't seem affected by Noah's passion.

"That is an interesting theory," Prosecutor mused, "but there is something I don't understand. How have the Phibs exerted so much effort in protecting the Lie? I can see how the creation of organized religion played a part in protecting it, but religion was not the only element shaping human morality. As Man evolved, he started to learn more about how he came to be. He realized Adam and Eve were a myth, so he turned to science to discover the truth explaining how he evolved. He discovered the human being as a mere product of biological and environmental evolution. So tell me, Noah, how does science fit into the protection of the Lie?"

Here is where I will shine, Noah thought, *my one understood truth*.

"That is much easier to explain than proving how organized religion is a protector of the Lie. I am referring to the one book having as much impact on human evolution of thought as the Bible. This would be the book by Charles Darwin, called *The Origin of the Species by Means of Natural Selection*."

"Aha," Prosecutor shouted. "I knew this book would make an appearance."

"Yes," Noah laughed. "How could it not?"

"Okay," Prosecutor said, "tell me Darwin's story."

"Darwin posed natural selection as a process of adaptations. He recognized that when environmental conditions are favorable, allowing the survival of all offspring, the number of individuals in a population would increase. He also knew that a population hardly ever realizes its biological potential for growth because of elements serving to control population growth. He referred to this as *environmental resistance*.

"Because of biological potential and environmental resistance, Darwin deduced that many offspring die as a result of a *struggle for survival.*

"Based on his observations, Darwin concluded that individual variations exist in all populations and species, and he further understood that the differences, which are inherited, were essential to his theory. He determined that the success of an individual was not measured simply in terms of physical strength, but more in terms of one's own ability to leave offspring. He referred to this ability as *fitness.*

"Darwin concluded that evolution occurred through a gradual change in the hereditary makeup of a species, and believed that the process of natural selection operates on rates of reproduction. It does not act directly on any other characteristic. Selection may act indirectly on other characteristics such as behavioral traits, but only through their effect on reproduction.

"In essence, biological characteristics evolve through their effect on reproduction."

"Basically," Prosecutor interrupted, "individuals grow, reproduce, and die."

"Yes, exactly, so when looking at this general summation of *Darwin's Theory of Evolution*, you would have to agree that there is nothing arrogant about the design of evolution. It is both logical and natural, ensuring that species can go on to the next generation. There is no emotion attached to it, and no indication of one species being superior and more deserving than another. Would you not agree?"

"Yes, it is a well-constructed way of survival."

"As the Phibs studied Darwin's findings," Noah continued, "they realized that to shield the truth from the masses, they had to determine how the evolutionary process of the animal life could be used to protect their precious Lie. The feature most often cited by the Phibs attempting to justify their moral and social views with science is the concept known as *survival of the fittest.* This application of Darwinian doctrine to human society and behavior is known as *Social Darwinism.*"

Suddenly Steven Biko rose from his seat and said, "I object."

As he turned to walk away, Sitting Bull stood and moved toward him, placing his hand over Mr. Biko's heart.

"Give him a chance," Prosecutor said, "he has yet to disappoint us."

Mr. Biko nodded, and he and Sitting Bull returned to their seats.

They are an impatient jury, Noah thought.

"Resume your testimony," Prosecutor ordered.

Noah complied.

"One of the most horrific features of Darwin's evolutionary theory was that it spawned comparisons between the *highest* and *lowest* human. Black people and native people were among the first to be singled out."

Sitting Bull and Mr. Biko gave each other an all-knowing look.

"Some anthropologists falsified their data to prove the "superiority" of the white race. There were anthropologists intentionally exaggerating the size of Caucasian skulls, and underestimating the size of black and native peoples' skulls, to provide manufactured evidence supporting the outrageously false suggestion that brain size has something to do with intelligence.

"Thus, Social Darwinism came to serve as scientific justification for racism."

"Humans are a mischievous race," Prosecutor remarked.

"Yes, that we are, but unfortunately it didn't stop there."

"How do you mean?"

"Well," Noah replied, "as with any theory put forth, it can often take on a life of its own."

"I think you had better clarify that statement."

"Darwin's science was not the only science applied to society," Noah said. "For example, Frances Galton, a cousin of Darwin's, founded the *Eugenics Movement*, the science seeking to improve the biological makeup of the human species. Galton believed that if controlled breeding was applied to humans, as it was to farm animals, a perfect human breed could be developed.

"It was this theory put into place by Adolph Hitler in an effort to create his twisted idea of the perfect human race. This race was called the *master race*, or the *pure Aryan race*.

"Benito Mussolini, who brought fascism to Italy, was also a great supporter of Darwinism. He strongly supported the belief that violence was an essential evolutionary trait.

"Therefore, by looking at the beliefs adopted from both science and religion, we can see how those embracing the self-deception gene, have managed to protect the Lie for so many generations."

Noah rose and approached the blackboard. If he had not been aware of the possible implications that may result from the outcome of the trial, he thought that he would be enjoying himself.

"Now," Noah said, "I will illustrate what resulted from the embracement of the evil gene; in other words, what cultivated from it."

Violence

Oppression		*Self-Preservation*
Racism		*Sadistic Behavior*
	←*Evil Gene*→	
Genocide		*Superiority Complex*
Slavery		*Insanity*
	Suffering	

Noah turned and faced the Jury.

"My argument is as follows: The evil gene was willingly injected into the human consciousness by the Phibs in an effort to maintain control over the Aphibs. There is no connection between the Creator and this gene. The evil gene itself is a manifestation of human weakness, the catalyst of a further modification in the human genetic makeup—the replacement of the morals and ethics forming the basis of human life.

"I will now illustrate the replacement."

→*Phibs*

Free Will →Lie →Self-Deception Gene →Hate →Evil Gene.

Immorality

Prosecutor and the Jury carefully studied the diagram while Noah returned to his seat.

"Immorality can be described as evil and sadistic principles of human evolution adopted and implemented by a group of Phibs. The purpose: To gain control of the process of evolution.

"Once the Phibs adopted immorality as the framework of human existence, they completely abandoned the original evolutionary process; in other words, they became self-created. Once self-created, the original Creator of the universe ceased to exist for this group.

"Therefore, the Creator is not responsible for their actions. They alone are responsible."

"Hmm," Prosecutor said, "when I look at your overall interpretation of the evolution of the evil gene, I have only one question: Why should such a species, who knowingly and selfishly chose a path of immorality, be allowed to continue to exist?"

"Well," Noah replied, "because the arguments that I have presented to you are only the tip of the iceberg. They don't explain the evolution of the entire human race. There are several other paths of human evolution, and as I will show you, evolution of the human mind is not one specific evolutionary path."

"You have given us a lot of information to absorb, but before we embark on another path of human evolution, I believe this would be an appropriate time for another recess."

Noah was captured by the Light.

iv.

"Hi, Noah."

Aidan was beaming.

"Hi," Noah said as he walked up to the sandbox. "I think I know how the crew of the *USS Enterprise* felt when they traveled through the transporter."

Aidan giggled, revealing his breathtaking spirit. He had completed his sand castle, and it was a work of art. In front, a bridge had been constructed with a door etched onto the wall where the bridge greeted it. He was now beginning to dig a shallow moat. Noah watched his small hands work the sand. He had never seen Aidan with such determination. He admired his dedication.

"What do you think?" Aidan asked.

" I think it's perfect."

"Oh, I don't think it is perfect, but it is pretty good. Now, come help me finish digging the moat."

Noah got down on his hands and knees and started to dig.

"I want to talk to you about Mom," Aidan said.

"Okay."

"All of your life, you resented Mom's spirituality. You thought that she was weak because she chose to believe, even though it gave her peace. It helped her deal with my death, and it will help her deal with the loss of Dad. Her spirituality gives her inner strength. Why would you think this was such a bad thing?"

He really goes right for the jugular, Noah thought.

"I believed she worshipped a fantasy and thought that false hope was a negative ideal."

"And now that you have had this experience, how do you feel about her beliefs?"

"Well...I still think her beliefs are misguided."

"Okay," he said. "I want you to think about all of her discussions about God. Did she ever tell us we were better than anyone else?"

Noah thought for a moment. He remembered the times when his Mom would tuck him into bed, wrap her arms around him, and whisper "I love you, and God loves you," in his ear. She smelled like homemade bread.

"No."

"Did she ever tell you that God sanctioned certain instances of murder and condoned slavery?"

"No."

"Now correct me if I'm wrong, but the memories I have of Mom's notions about God are that he is an all-loving and all-good being who suffered when we suffered, and cried when we cried. I don't remember her telling us that God physically protects us. She said that if we believed in God, our souls would never be harmed, and in spite of all of the evil things people do to one another in the world, if we remain true to God, our souls would always remain his."

"Yes, but that seemed so silly at the time."

Aidan started to laugh, "But now that you have come here, what do you think of her beliefs about God?"

"Well..."

Noah reflected for a moment, trying to think of something negative to say. He couldn't.

"I guess her interpretation of God was virtuous."

"Yes, she believed in an all-good being and expected nothing material from him in return. She chose to believe in a higher goodness, and chose not to judge you when you denounced his existence. She allowed you to make your own choices in life, and permitted you to believe what you wanted when you were old enough to make the decision for yourself. She brought us to church to introduce us to spirituality. All she ever wanted was to instill important sentiments such as love, respect, and peace. She tried to teach us that amidst an angry world, there was another choice."

"Yeah," Noah sighed, "she was cool about it."

Aidan giggled and said, "Cool."

"I guess it would be okay to say that Mom did not have an ulterior motive for taking us to church," he continued. "She just wanted to expose us to another aspect of humanity."

"Yeah."

Noah reflected on her spirituality. It was so peaceful; there was never any anger in her eyes. Noah scratched his head, wondering why he never saw it before. The walls started to crumble.

"So how can you find fault with her beliefs?"

"I can't. I just didn't look at it that way before."

"I guess you only saw what you wanted to see."

"Yes," Noah sighed, "I guess I did."

"How do you feel about it now?"

Noah thought about it and blushed.

"I guess I feel like an ungrateful idiot."

Aidan burst into laughter.

"Don't be so hard on yourself, Noah. It was your chosen destiny."

As Noah opened his mouth to reply, the Light intervened.

The Sinking of Noah's Ark

Chapter VII

Prosecutor's grin expressed excitement about the next round. Noah hoped that he would not disappoint him. He looked around the room and noticed something different about it. It didn't seem to be so cold, and the walls were much brighter. It was as if someone had cleaned them during his absence. Noah was feeling more at ease, more in tune with his senses.

"When we last adjourned," Prosecutor said, "I believe that you were about to take us on another journey down the evolutionary road of life, down a path devoid of the evil gene. It's a path that you feel will explain the essence of humanity. You have the court's undivided attention, Noah; please proceed with your argument."

Noah cleared his throat. "As I mentioned in our last session, human evolution hasn't evolved as an entirety. Because of intellect and free will, Man had the ability to choose which evolutionary path to take. In order to explain the alternate path, I would like to return to the original evolutionary process."

He paused to wait for an interruption, but there was none. Prosecutor remained seated.

"In spite of the greater majority," Noah continued, "not every Phib chose to adopt the Lie. The majority of people who believe in God don't commit evil acts. Through intellect and free will, there were those who chose to stray from the evolution of the evil gene when the Lie was created, and from that point on the evolutionary process was altered; in other words, another branch grew."

Noah rose and walked to the blackboard.

"I will demonstrate the change of course in my diagram."

→*Phibs*

Free Will → *Morality* → <u>*Selfish Gene*</u> → *Lie* → *Self-Deception Gene*

Unconditional Acceptance

Returning to his seat, Noah continued with his testimony.

"There were a group of Phibs, from the myths passed down throughout generations, accepting the ideals associated with God as the truth. They adopted the beliefs and morals of God without questioning its validity. The believers chose to follow the Phibs' original interpretation of God and did so by adopting the guidelines set out in the Scriptures, which in turn served as their foundation of morals and ethics. Basically, their beliefs ended with the phrase: *God is great, God is good. Thank you, God, for this food.*"

Prosecutor chuckled. "That's simplistic."

"Yeah," Noah said, "it is a simplistic belief."

"But that doesn't seem like such a terrible way of worshipping God," Prosecutor added.

"Yes, initially it appears that way, but it's my argument that those who don't question don't learn, and without learning, how can one evolve? Learning is one of the major elements forming the essence of the evolutionary process of the mind. If we stop learning, how can we evolve to a higher state of consciousness?"

"True," Prosecutor remarked.

"Fortunately," Noah continued, "adopting the Lie was not written in stone, although a myth was created testifying to the Lie. Anyway, an intellectual and freethinking species such as Man had the ability study the Lie and rationalize that there were some problems with it. This included doubting racist views and the belief that God put Man on Earth to rule the planet, taking as much from it as he wanted. In spite of the flaws, they refused to embrace the evil gene, and from this unconditional acceptance, another branch sprouted in the process."

Noah rose and made his way to the blackboard.

→*Phibs*

Free Will →Lie →Unconditional Acceptance

Conditional Acceptance

"How did conditional acceptance evolve?" Prosecutor asked.

"Conditional acceptance came about after generations of learning and forming individual ideas and beliefs that were separate from the original code of ethics. The atrocities committed by those embracing the evil gene resulted in many Phibs going back and reexamining their initial beliefs about God. Phib still believed in the original ideals associated with God, but realized that too much arrogance was not spiritual.

"So, Phib began sharing his ideas with others. People started to look at the world as a product of Man straying away from God in a self-serving quest for power. It is these individuals who began to look at the world around them and say to themselves: *Hey, I think there are a few things that need to be fixed.* They decided to correct some of the problems in order to make the world a better place."

" So," Prosecutor interrupted, "an example would be individuals who first engaged in such tasks as helping the poor, working to overcome racism, saving your natural resources, helping people in the Third World Countries...etcetera."

"Yes, they realized Man can be remarkably cruel when he wants to be, and in spite of history, they attempted to maintain their belief in God by undoing Phib's selfish deeds. They accepted the Lie, but realized there were some flaws with the original interpretation of morality."

Noah paused and then announced, "Now, I will illustrate the process." He said this as though he were about to reveal the secrets of the universe.

→*Phibs*

Lie →Unconditional Acceptance →Doubt →Conditional Acceptance

Morality

Returning to his seat, he glanced at the blank faces of the Jury and resumed his testimony.

"In their reality, the unconditional acceptors were attempting to create a basis of morality that was not founded entirely on arrogance and selfishness. They started to realize that other races were not inferior to them, and those who believed so had some fundamental flaws in their ideals. Therefore, my argument is as follows: The evolution of the human race did not result in a species where all are evil.

"As evolution continued, there were those within the species who discovered, through spiritual growth, logical reasoning and an evolving intellect, that the evolutionary path chosen by Man needed some adjustments. From this doubt came a new group of people attempting to live a moral and ethical life, and they still do. They realized that living a life based on arrogance and selfishness was detrimental to the future of their species, as well as the other species."

Prosecutor and the Jury studied the diagram while Noah's stomach did somersaults.

"So," Prosecutor blared, "Man didn't completely screw up the process of evolution because there were those choosing to break free from Man's original designed destiny. There were individuals who discovered that the truth they believed in may not be the whole truth."

"Yes, and this fact supports my theory that Man, a result of the process of evolution, is not a purely evil product. Therefore, God cannot be found guilty of creating a universe with an evolutionary process that resulted in the creation of an all-evil species. Evil people have been created, but they are self-created. The original Creator of the universe did not play a role in their creation."

Noah was not sure how Prosecutor interpreted the words, but he thought they sounded good coming out of his mouth.

Prosecutor grinned and said, "Basically, you are saying that you don't all live in a yellow submarine."

"Yes," Noah laughed, "the submarine was decommissioned once water became a marketable product."

He smiled and Noah returned the smile. For an odd reason, Prosecutor's acceptance was becoming important to him.

"I understand how conditional acceptance emerged," Prosecutor said, "but I'm unsure of this unconditional acceptance theory. Are you saying that everyone who initially accepted the Lie unconditionally eventually evolved to a state of conditional acceptance? Because if you are, I can clearly cite numerous examples proving otherwise."

"No, of course not. If that were true, then the world would be a much better place. Those who accepted the Lie unconditionally have remained true to their faith, even now, but to understand the role of the unconditional acceptors in history, you have to look at how their thought processes evolved."

Noah proceeded to the blackboard.

"This group of individuals did not just pause in the evolutionary process, they too evolved to another state of consciousness."

While picking up the chalk, Noah told Prosecutor and the Jury that he would demonstrate the process.

→*Phibs*

Free Will →Lie →Unconditional Acceptance →Conditional Acceptance

Morally Impaired

He walked back to his seat, glancing at Prosecutor and the Jury. Their eyes were fixed on the blackboard.

"It is the morally impaired who unfortunately make up the majority of the population. They retain morals and ethics, believing hate, murder, and prejudice are wrong. That's moral, right?"

"Yes, that's moral," Prosecutor laughed.

"But the fundamental flaw is that their moral ideals are only applied to those residing within their borders. This flaw leads to the story of the *Haves, Have-Nots* and *Have Less*."

"This is a story that you will now share with the court?"

"Yes," Noah replied. "You see, the morally impaired have accepted certain problems in the world as a permanent and normal condition. For instance, they have come to accept human suffering as a fact of life. One example would be the famine and disease preying upon people of the Third World, leaving behind millions of deaths each year. It has become morally accepted. Therefore, my argument is as follows: The world as one mass consciousness has moved from morality to that of being morally impaired. Suffering in the Have-Not countries has become an accepted truth emerging from the Lie.

"Now, when I channel surf on the television, I am confronted with a couple from the Have world being rewarded for producing eight babies in one birth, and these births have resulted from science.

"In essence, the Phibs have taken over the reproductive aspect of the evolutionary process to serve their own selfish desires."

"Aha," Prosecutor shouted. "Again we see Darwin's Survival of the Fittest regime rearing its ugly head."

"Exactly. The Haves have now adopted the belief that those residing in the Have Countries are more deserving than those living in the Have-Not world. This is an institutionalized code of morality readily implemented and accepted by the Haves. As the Haves mobilize and take complete control of the world's resources, the Have-Not countries become irrelevant. Those who 'have' have become desensitized to the suffering and death in the Have-Not world. They have developed the ability to view a starving child on the television and feel nothing. *It is your fault*, the Haves say, *you shouldn't be breeding so much.*

"Instead of trying to understand why there has been such a large population increase, they conclude that it's stupidity."

"What should the Haves understand?"

"Setting aside cultural beliefs as a factor, in a world where human life can be dreadfully brief, the Have-Nots are trying to extend a part of themselves in hopes that their offspring will have a better and longer life. The Have-Nots are trying to ensure that their generation doesn't become extinct. It's the only survival instinct they have left.

"The Haves take it upon themselves to look down from their ivory towers and judge the Have-Nots' survival method, denying any responsibility, although they continue to pollute the earth and perpetuate global warming, causing the land of the Have-Nots to shrivel and die.

"The Have-Nots are left begging for scraps as the Almighty Haves shake their all-knowing fingers at them and say *Tisk, Tisk.*

"The tragic flaw of the Haves is this: They have taken it upon themselves to judge the Have-Nots according to their own interpretation of morality, even if it is hypocritical."

"What do you mean by hypocritical?"

"Some of the Haves, armed with their degrees, believe that the world should allow nature to take its course in regards to the increased population; that is, allowing people in these countries to die from famine and disease, since that is how nature deals with overpopulation. They say it is natural, but let's pose for instance that one of these scholarly Haves is skiing down a steep mountain. As you know, avalanches are common. Now, imagine an avalanche occurs while the Have is making his way down the hill, and he is completely engulfed and covered by twenty feet of snow. Would the Have say: *Gosh, I am the unfortunate victim of a natural occurrence. Although I am alive at the moment, I hope no one risks his life to save me. Because my situation is the result of a natural occurrence, I should be left to die.*

Prosecutor laughed. "I would imagine the Have would scream bloody murder for someone to come and rescue him."

"Exactly, and why do you think so many Have-Nots stow away on boats, crammed in tiny compartments, often succumbing to thirst, hunger, and suffocation in an effort to reach the Have world? Because they believe that if they succeed, they will be able to assimilate themselves into the Have world, and share in the wealth and freedoms the Haves control and trickle down upon the masses."

"You are saying," Prosecutor interrupted, "that in the Have world today, it has become morally acceptable that one person can be a multi-millionaire, while another slowly and painfully wastes away to nothing but a bag of bones."

Prosecutor fell silent, revealing a puzzled look on his face. Noah asked him what was the matter.

"I am unclear about something. The Have countries you discuss—is everyone living there considered a Have?"

"No, of course not," Noah replied. "In the world of the Haves, the Haves make up a small percentage of the population, and the rest of the population can be considered the Have-Less. You see, The Haves have created an ingenious illusion within their own borders: To Have or to Have Not is the fundamental philosophy embodying the Have world. The Haves have instilled the ideal that to 'have' is the ultimate purpose in life, and to accumulate the useless items that the Haves bombard them with is how the Have-Less achieve glorified Have status. These items are irrelevant to the Have-Less' survival and happiness, but the Have-Less have been trained well. They have come to believe that if they fill their homes with these items, they will be self-fulfilled."

"But the Have-Less can't afford such luxuries," Prosecutor countered.

"Of course," Noah said. "But the Haves have created an ingenious method of extracting blood from a turnip: the development and use of credit cards, loans, and the like. It ensures that the Have-Less are prevented from moving into Have neighborhoods."

"But since the Haves are just as dependent on the Have-Less, wouldn't messing with them be an unwise decision?"

"Yes, it would be. Of course the Haves, being full aware of their dependence on the Have-Less, realize that their world would come crashing down around them if the Have-Less woke up one day and decided they no longer needed the Haves' products, so the Haves devised a method to ensure this does not happen. Basically, they had to manipulate the Have-Less way of thinking."

"How did they achieve such a remarkable feat?"

"By instilling their own set of values into Have-Less culture. The fundamental value: Without an abundance of material goods, your life is meaningless.

"The information medium became the key to instilling these ideals. The Haves now had ample means of telling the masses that buying more goods will somehow make them better human beings. In other words, excessive selfishness is morally acceptable."

"How has the information medium been successful in affecting thought patterns?"

"Well," Noah replied, "through this medium, the Haves now control the Have-Less way of interpreting the world. The Haves can tell the Have-Less what to believe, what to wear, and what products are best for them. The Haves have been able to instruct the Have-Less on how to live, essentially becoming the authors of the Have-Less' story."

"How do they present the world to the Have Less?"

"The view of the world is portrayed in three-minute sound bytes with the bigger picture, becoming lost in a sea of hazy images. Even such acts as war have been electronically controlled to make the Have-Less believe what the Haves want them to."

"Can you expand on your war example?"

"Yes," Noah replied. "War has been transformed into a video game with journalists, once respected truth-seekers, now nothing more than sportscasters, reporting the number of deaths like points in a boxing match. The Have-Less sit glued in front of their television sets watching the captivating missiles streak across the sky. They never wonder who lies dead at the end of the target; whose mother, father, sister, or brother. The bodies, scattered across the bloody streets, represent points scored by the other team, and it is just a game as long as it is kept away from Have shores. The Have-Less sit and wait in anticipation of the next round."

"What is the message?" Prosecutor asked.

"The fundamental message received by the Have-Less: *My life could be worse. I should be thankful for where I live and what I have got. I had better not complain.* This realization has manifested itself into a new emotion, *joyless self-contentment*, a feeling now expressed by the masses. It has become a state of consciousness, a pause in our mental evolution."

"It would explain the increased use of antidepressants."

"Yes," Noah said.

"Are you saying that this pause in the evolution of the mind is preventing the human race from improving the world?"

"Yes, the masses of Have-Less have created their own sense of reality. They live their lives through the electronic boob-tube, willingly absorbing the information presented to them, freely accepting it as the truth, never doubting its validity or those spoon-feeding it to them."

Prosecutor scratched his head and the Jury looked at each other with baffled expressions. Noah started to worry his testimony was not making an impact.

"I understand," Prosecutor said, "the argument about Man creating his own destiny through the choices that he made in life, but what I fail to see is any evidence demonstrating Man's understanding of the consequences of his choices."

Prosecutor expelled a deep, heartfelt sigh.

"After listening to your argument, I think it's fair to say that the evolution of the mind is a fact of life that cannot be stopped or reversed. You talk of the morally impaired as mass consciousness, but there are others living amongst the masses who seek to reverse the evolutionary process. They aren't content with a pause, and are moving on in deceitful ways: in the name of God, through propaganda, providing false data about other races, and recruiting weak individuals having financial and social difficulties. They convince themselves, and others, that it is the non-white, non-Christian and homosexuals that are responsible for their lack of success. All you have presented is Phib selfishly choosing a life of lies that ends up causing immense suffering. I don't see any goodness in human history."

Prosecutor paused and closed his eyes. For an instant, Noah thought that he was about to conclude the trial. After a moment of silence, he opened his eyes, rose from his seat, and approached him.

"Today," he said, "Have society has experienced a tremendous social change, ignited by the increase in immigration, the civil rights movement, the women's rights movement, and the gay and lesbian movement. Have society is now a luxurious basket of individuals.

"Many Phibs perceive the change as personal attacks. The shift to the right in Have politics, the increasing influence of Phib extremists, and the resurgence of biological explanations for racial inequality have provided a malicious environment for promoting the evil beliefs of Phib groups. Many Phibs argue that the playing field no longer exists, and discrimination is a myth. Programs attempting to increase opportunities for women and minorities are seen as providing them with an unfair advantage. For example, programs like affirmative action have been labeled 'reverse discrimination,' despite evidence indicating otherwise. A growing number of Phibs feel that they are an oppressed minority, and this feeling has led to the establishment of various Phib organizations determined to fight an imaginary war against evolution.

"Even more disturbing, some of these Phib organizations base themselves on religion. They use God to denounce other religions, and promote hatred. Why? Because they feel they know what the correct way to live is, and their race and religion are superior to all others."

Prosecutor started to pace back and forth in front of Noah, his hands clenched in tight fists. Noah wished he would call for another recess.

"Some of the organizations," Prosecutor continued, "feel that all non-white, non-Christian, and gay people should be eliminated, either through kicking them out of the country or killing them. Some Phibs attempt to exert their religious beliefs in other institutions such as schools. In fact, through their own ignorant fear, Phibs have revived the Lie. They are attempting to de-evolve society, and do so in the name of their God to acquire power and control."

He stopped and ran his fingers through his hair, his face strained and his eyes drooping. He glared at Noah.

"So, along with the morally impaired individuals, I contend that Phib's resurgence of his God is not a spiritual desire. It is a self-serving and greedy political motive. Phib is attempting to spread his evil gene for his own selfish purpose. There is no spirituality within these Phib organizations, as they are founded on hate, and their morals and ethics are based on immorality. They are doing so in the name of their values, and to hell with everyone else's values. They sound like someone we both know—Hitler.

"Can you explain why Man has yet to obtain higher consciousness? With such beliefs still flourishing in your world, do you not think it is about time for the Creator to say: *Enough, this species is incapable of growing. They had more than one chance to fix themselves. It's time to rid the world of such evil.*"

Prosecutor returned to his seat, folded his arms across his chest, and stared at Noah.

"Ah," Noah exclaimed. "This is where I can prove the true strength of humanity."

"How so?" Prosecutor asked bitterly. "I cannot see it."

"I understand why you can't see it; you aren't the only one. The problem is that the truth is often masked by the results of the Lies. If you look through the pain and suffering that has occurred throughout human history, you will see a truth overpowering the Lie, but the evil has been so devastating, it often overshadows this truth.

"The tragic part of the truth is the past atrocities inflicted by the evil gene in an effort to bury it, but as I will show you, this truth was not, and will not be, buried. Too many minds have been infected with the truth, so that the majority will eventually, I hope, reveal the Lie. I believe the truth has remained and taken on an evolutionary path of its own."

"You are referring to the self-realization gene that you put in your little human evolution chart."

Little, Noah thought. *That's condescending.*

"Yes."

"Okay", he said, "but before we go down that path, I believe it's time for another recess. The Jury and I wish to analyze the dark side of humanity that you have presented thus far."

1:

As Noah approached the sandbox, Aidan was sitting complacently in front of the castle. His project was complete. The moat had been carefully excavated around the fortress, and a bridge was erected to allow safe passage to the castle doors. Every tiny detail of the castle was meticulously etched, not one grain of sand was out of place. It was magnificent. Noah cautiously sat beside him so as not to disturb his creation.

"It's done," Aidan announced proudly.

"I can see that," Noah said. "It's remarkable."

He giggled and bowed his head bashfully.

"Thank you," he said. "I'm glad you came back, because I still have something I want to talk to you about."

"Okay, shoot."

"I want to talk to you about knowledge."

"Knowledge?"

"Yes, knowledge. I remember spending a great deal of time in your room. I loved looking at all of your books. I couldn't understand them, but you did."

"Yes."

"Well," Aidan continued, "now, when I reflect on those books, I realize that each book told a story, each story had an author, and each author had a message for the reader."

"Yes, that's true."

"And the message, in the author's opinion, was how things came to be."

"Yes."

"This knowledge is powerful, as it formed the core of your future and served as your crutch in life."

He paused and looked at Noah, his eyes fixed on his. The rich blueness penetrated Noah, demanding something from him.

"Noah, how is that so different from the Bible?"

Noah had to think for a moment. Aidan was much more challenging than his university professors.

"Well," he replied, "my books gave me the knowledge of the concrete, knowledge with facts to support it."

"But this knowledge shaped your thoughts and beliefs."

"Yes, it did."

"And this knowledge was written by a human, as was the Bible."

"Yes, but there are clearly different messages being presented."

"The message is irrelevant," Aidan said. "What is important is how you perceive the message. I mean, how you perceive the world."

"True."

Noah stared at him. He was filled with respect for his baby brother.

"As we have already discussed," Aidan said, "you are prone to both selfish and arrogant tendencies.

"Yes." Noah blushed, wondering when Aidan was going to make his point.

"And you now know how these tendencies can alter one's pattern of thought."

"Yes," Noah replied.

"This means that you aren't that different from anyone else."

Noah reflected on his words, unable to think of a good response.

"I suppose not," he reluctantly replied.

"So, the opinions and beliefs that you embraced contain some flaws."

"Yes, I guess so."

Aidan paused, revealing a powerful smile.

"Well," he declared, "I guess there's only thing left to do."

On that note, Aidan stood, cast Noah a devilish look, and without warning, began kicking and smashing the castle.

"What are you doing?" Noah shouted.

He laughed and continued the demolition until there were no remaining signs of the castle. Noah sat in disbelief.

"Why did you destroy it? You worked so hard to build it."

Aidan looked at Noah, beaming with joy.

Pointing to the sand, he laughed and said, "Look, Noah."

"Look at what?"

"It's not gone," he replied triumphantly.

Aidan picked up a handful of sand and tossed it into the air, sprinkling over Noah.

"It's there," Aidan said, "it has always been there. As long as there is sand in the box, it will always be there."

He stopped suddenly and gazed at Noah; a beautiful smile emerged. He ran over to him, wrapped his arms tightly around him, and planted a huge kiss on his cheek. Noah felt his heart break.

Before he could respond, the dreadful Light advanced upon him.

Aidan's final words to his brother drifted after him: "I love you, Noah."

The Sinking of Noah's Ark

Chapter VIII

Prosecutor was mindlessly tapping his fingers on the table, his face more relaxed. Noah had come to appreciate the recesses.

"Well, Noah," he said, "at this point in the game, the trial will be taking on a much different format. In your previous testimony, you presented sufficient evidence suggesting how Man has taken on an evil role in the evolutionary process, but now the floor is open to you. You have the difficult task of proving humanity itself is not evil."

Noah immediately thought of Aidan hurling the sand into the air and grinned.

"Okay."

"From what you have argued so far," Prosecutor continued, "you believe that the evolution of the human psyche includes both recognizing and realizing Man's belief system is flawed. It is through learning that Man is supposed to evolve to a higher state of consciousness. This involves embracing the self-realization gene.

"I don't believe Man has done this, and can't see it from what you have said so far, but I will give you the benefit of the doubt and listen to your arguments."

Well this is really good, Noah thought. *I made it through the darkest part of humanity. Now all I have to do is expose Man's goodness. I hope it's possible.*

An image of his mother flashed in his mind.

Noah rose and walked to the blackboard. He turned to face Prosecutor and the Jury.

"In order to understand the self-realization gene, I will illustrate its course in an evolutionary chart."

Noah picked up the chalk and proceeded:

→*Phibs*

Free Will → *Morality* → <u>*Selfish Gene*</u> → *Lie* → *Self Deception Gene*

Aphibs   Truth

Self Realization Gene → *Morality*

Returning to his seat, Noah observed Prosecutor and the Jury carefully studying the diagram.

"You have cited just a few examples of the horrible atrocities committed by those allowing the evil gene to infect them, but I will now argue that the self-deception gene is not an essential element of human DNA. In other words, the gene was not necessary in ensuring that human evolution would continue.

"I intend to prove that Man was not designed to be evil, and that the evil he embraced, he did by choice. I will do this by revealing the many people who refused to accept the Lie as a foundation of morality. There are people throughout human history who willingly defied the Lie, although it meant suffering the wrath of the evil gene.

"Basically, I'm going to tell you the story of the Aphibs."

Noah paused and looked at the Jury. They were leaning back in their chairs, listening carefully.

"Through the deep, hideous images of the past," he began, " a glimmer of light always appears. The light is so powerful that the evil gene could never have extinguished it, and no matter how hard the evil gene tried, and still tries, it cannot be done. The light is so strong that the evil gene has committed many horrific acts in fear of it.

"After every horrible event that has taken place in human history, the light appears. I contend that the light belongs to those having fought, died, and survived the wrath of the evil gene.

"I will now enter into evidence instances proving the existence of this light. First, I will discuss the most infamous atrocity known to Man—the Jewish Holocaust.

"As you are well aware, the activities in concentration camps consisted of torture, rape, horrific medical experiments, starvation, disease, and mass genocide, particularly in the gas chambers.

"When anyone from my era reads about the events, or sees the documentary evidence, he would likely say: *I could have never made it.* The condition emanated hopelessness. They could have all committed suicide to escape the Nazi wrath, and yes, some did, which I believe can be seen as a form of resistance."

"Resistance?" Prosecutor interrupted.

"Yes, my best interpretation: When some of the prisoners looked at the situation around them, and realized no one was coming to liberate them, they decided the best way to defeat the Nazis was to end their lives before the Nazis could do it for them. By doing so, they were saying to their captors, *You have no control over my fate. I will not submit to your will.*"

"Ah," Prosecutor said, "I can see that. But why did you say 'my best interpretation?'"

"I wasn't there. I don't know the pain."

Prosecutor glanced at Einstein, and Einstein nodded to him.

Turning his attention to Noah, he said, "Good. Continue."

"But there were others, in spite of the hopelessness of the situation and the immense suffering endured on a daily basis, choosing to resist. There are many instances of armed and spiritual resistance in the death camps and the ghettos. Those choosing armed resistance had many methods, such as violent and confrontational defiance. They also resisted through petitions, protection payments, and ransom payments, and some chose to comply with anti-Jew laws to prevent persecution; that is, to stay alive.

"In the ghettos, all forms of culture preserved life. Praying was against the rules, but Synagogue services were still held. The education of children was forbidden, but ghetto communities set up schools organized to meet religious, educational, and cultural needs. Some Jews escaped death by hiding in attics, cellars, and closets of non-Jews. Also, writings and oral histories of survivors of the labor and concentration camps are filled with accounts of sabotage.

"More than twelve million people perished in the war; more than six million were Jews. You would think that sort of persecution would have made them all give up, but they didn't. Survivors emerged. I argue that it takes more than just basic survival instincts to make it through such a horrific event. It is something more powerful inside driving a person in those circumstances to fight for survival. I can't completely understand it, because I have never been in a situation where I had to find this inner strength, but it's something so powerful, it goes beyond the basic instincts of survival. I contend that the survivors are evidence that the truth exists, and what sprouted from this truth is the essence of humanity, divided into two branches of morality.

I will illustrate my argument in my human evolution chart."

Noah approached the blackboard and picked up the chalk:

→. *Iphibs*

Free Will →Truth →Self Realization Gene →Unknowing . Itheism →True Creator

He returned to his seat and observed Prosecutor, pen in mouth, staring thoughtfully at the diagram.

"What links the unknowing atheist to the true Creator is the realization that God was created in an image of the Phibs to perpetuate the Lie, and as a means of embracing the evil gene so Phib could live a life of immorality."

"Do the survivors represent the two branches of morality?"

"Yes. One would think that those walking out of the camps would have all denounced the existence of a higher power, and with good reason, many did. But there were others who maintained their beliefs. There are noted instances of men and women marching to the death camps chanting, *I believe with perfect faith in the coming of the Messiah.* Also, researchers asked survivors of the death camps how they could believe in God after Auschwitz. Some said that they had entered the camp as a religious Jew, and nothing had changed their beliefs."

"Their faith survived," Prosecutor interrupted. "Their faith in God was a source of strength, helping them survive."

"Yes, so my argument is as follows: The God that the survivors sought strength from is not the same God created out of arrogance. The God they believed in is actually the true Creator, and that became the final defeat of Hitler.

"The destruction of Hitler and his regime was more than just a military act, as there was one aspect of human nature the Nazis could not destroy: in spiritual terms, the soul, and in unknowing atheist terms, the essence of humanity.

"By repopulating and maintaining their faith, Hitler failed. The self-realization gene overpowered the evil gene in its never-ending struggle."

"From what you have just cited," Prosecutor interrupted, "I believe there is an important lesson to be learned. The Phibs are capable of committing any act, no matter how horrible and evil it is. If Phib can conceive it, he can and will do it."

"Yes," Noah said. "It's my argument that the evil gene leaves behind so much devastation and pain on its journey of immorality, the truth is often concealed."

As he paused to catch a second wind, Prosecutor started to open his mouth. Noah quickly cut in.

"Before you respond, I would like to enter into evidence further examples of the presence of the self-realization gene. It will show that the truth has been in existence for as long as the Lie, therefore making the argument that Man is inherently an evil product of evolution false."

Prosecutor grinned. "You have my undivided attention."

"I would now like to discuss a group of people historically mistreated, enslaved, tortured, and murdered. I will tell you the story of the people of Africa."

Steven Biko leaned back in his chair, resting his elbows on the arms.

"Most of the Africans abducted by slave traders came from an area bordering the west coast of Africa," Noah began. "They were taken in chains from thousands of villages and towns. The prisoners were purchased from brokers at forts, factories or in open markets. When they were received, they were stripped and thoroughly examined by doctors. Those deemed healthy had the mark of the French, English, or Dutch companies burned into their flesh. The prisoners, branded and in chains, were then taken to the slave ships for the horrid passage across the Atlantic Ocean.

"On the boats, prisoners were crammed into tiny compartments in the hull. During the long passage, they were beaten, murdered and raped. When the ships arrived in the United States, the prisoners were sold to plantation owners and forced into slavery.

"On most plantations, overseers and drivers ruled with brutal force. Rapes, murders, and whippings were an everyday occurrence. One would think that under such horrific conditions, the men, women, and children who were forcibly taken from their homes in Africa would see their situation as hopeless, and either accept their life, or commit suicide in defiance of their cruel masters."

"Yes," Prosecutor interrupted, "one would think that."

"But they didn't," Noah continued. "In spite of the greater majority oppressing them, they resisted. History is laced with many incidents of slave revolts, and there were many instances of individual struggle. For example, in

1849, Harriet Tubman escaped slavery in Maryland. Returning to the South nineteen times, she brought out more than thirty slaves. She did this in spite of great risk to herself, an example of the survival instinct evolving to higher consciousness.

"On the plantations, resistance was common. Slaves poisoned their masters and mistresses, and burned the houses, distilleries, and barns to the ground. They also destroyed crops, farm equipment, and stole silver and wine.

"There were also instances of passive resistance. *Slaves would neither smile nor bow to their captors, work no harder than they had to, stage sit-down strikes, and flee to swamps at cotton-picking time.*"

"You have cited good examples," Prosecutor said, "but life was no picnic for black people even after the abolishment of slavery."

"Yes, the examples that I cited are just a few instances of resistance before the Emancipation Proclamation. Following the Civil War, black people were no longer slaves, but were legally separated from whites. Segregation began as a method to control black people because slavery was no longer permitted in the United States. For years, black people suffered at the hands of the hate groups. They were tortured and murdered in the most horrific ways, but they refused to be oppressed.

"To challenge the segregation laws, Civil Rights activists in the 1960's, held protest marches, boycotts, and refused to abide by segregation laws. Despite efforts of hate groups using threats, violence, and murder to defeat the activists, they persisted. After many highly publicized protests, and the Civil Rights march where Martin Luther King Jr. gave his infamous *I have a dream* speech, President John F. Kennedy Jr. proposed the new Civil Rights law.

"The Civil Rights movement put fundamental reforms in place. Legal segregation was dismantled, public institutions were open to all, and African-Americans could now vote."

"So, what is the lesson to be learned from your story?"

"Many people died for this cause, including Martin Luther King Jr., but the lesson to be learned about humanity is that when faced with adversity, those who keep the truth in their hearts—that is, those who refute the Lie—embrace the essence of humanity, or the soul. Racial inequality still exists, but the struggle continues, and no one gives up. The self-realization gene that has been passed down from generation to generation by those who suffered and died for freedom still exists. That is the power of the truth. No matter how many times in human history the evil gene sought to destroy it, it never succeeded. That is the heart of humanity."

"So," Prosecutor interjected, "you are arguing that no matter what reasons history buffs apply to the atrocities in human history, for example, religious, economic, or political motives, the remarkable feats the oppressed overcame cannot be attributed solely to the basic instinct of survival inherited through generations of evolution. The strength of the oppressed can be attributed to a higher consciousness of morality and spirituality."

"Exactly."

While making his way to the blackboard, Noah tells Prosecutor and the

Jury that he will demonstrate the process.

→ *Aphibs*

Arrogance →Free Will →Selfish Gene

Truth

Higher Consciousness ←Self Realization Gene →Higher Consciousness

Unknowing Atheism   *True Creator*

Prosecutor studied the diagram. He tipped his head to the right and scratched it.

"There are those believing that your genes have always been a part of you," he said, "and you were in fact designed to be a selfish species. In fact, it is your selfishness that defines you. For instance, there is a group of intellectuals known as *evolutionary psychologists* believing that Man has not evolved much since the Stone Age. They suggest that there are a number of factors that have prevented humans from evolving further: *First, the distribution of human beings all over the world has made genetic modifications difficult. Second, environmental changes have been minimal, prohibiting the need for further evolutions. And third, not enough time has passed for genetic mutations to occur.*

"So, in conclusion, Evolutionary psychologists believe that the human mind is designed in ways controlling most human behavior today."

Prosecutor hit a sore spot.

"I believe that's bullshit."

The Jury smiled while Prosecutor exploded into laughter.

Ignoring his outburst, he said, "Biologically speaking, Man may not have evolved due to those reasons, but the human mind is a much more complex system. Our tribal instincts have been blamed for our notorious history, and now they say our genes are responsible. That would be like saying the Nazis were not accountable for their actions because their genes dictated their actions, and it was evolution that created the genes.

"It is ludicrous to say our genes control us. I think it's a terrifying theory. The new trend of evolutionary psychology seeks to eliminate morality by degrading it to nothing but genetic selfishness."

"Then why is evolutionary psychology so popular?"

"Because it promises to replace morality with a more self-serving theory known as *scientific or technological morality*. Evolutionary psychologists claim that by examining the history of human evolution, we can identify behavior that has been selected and encoded in our DNA to provide an adaptive moral value. It is my argument that if this were true, then morality and free will are just an illusion. This trend of thinking is bogus. We are not mere circus animals performing at the brutal will of our enslaving genes.

"In an era where morality is at an all-time low, this fad seeks to replace morality based on religion with morality based on science, and I don't see much improvement to society if this philosophy is adopted by the masses."

"We have already discussed atrocities committed in the name of God," Prosecutor said. "Why couldn't morality based on science be an improvement?"

"This new scientific view of morality encourages and even promotes destructive and self-serving behavior. Man is no longer defined by his moral character. The measure of a man is now determined by how much power and wealth he acquires. Success combined with power and wealth has become morality itself. It is morality without meaning, known as *amorality*.

"Today, some evolutionary theorists claim that if they study animal behavior as it relates to natural selection, they can show how biological influences have produced a human species that is nothing more than devious genes pushing the behavioral buttons of a stupid species."

The Jury suddenly burst into laughter. Noah smiled and resumed.

"Animals survive on instinct, an established fact. Researchers have studied wolf packs in the wild working together to take down their prey. We now know how animals function as a society to survive, but what does that really tell us about the genocidal acts committed throughout human history? What does that tell us about human beings putting on white sheets and hanging other human beings from trees?

"My answer: Absolutely nothing."

Dian Fossey suddenly cleared her throat. Prosecutor and Noah glanced over at her. She was holding a piece of paper. Prosecutor walked over and retrieved it from her. While reading what she had written, he started to laugh and returned to his seat.

"So," Prosecutor said, "if your argument is to be found valid, then one could sum up your interpretation of evolutionary psychology by citing the famous line from William Faulkner's novel, The Sound and the Fury:

> *"Life is a tale told by an idiot,*
> *Full of sound and fury,*
> *Signifying nothing."*

"Yes," Noah laughed. "You hit the nail right on the head."

"Are you saying that studying animal behavior is a pointless endeavor?"

"No, I'm saying that researchers should stop coming up with ways to justify human immoral behavior by drawing ridiculous comparisons between species. Maybe they should try to discover how all of the other species in the world live without evil in their biological makeup. For instance, comparing the term selfishness with both a songbird protecting its nesting area, and a man who kills his wife because she no longer wants to be his property, is ludicrous. We have to realize that selfishness as it is applied to animals is much different than selfishness applied to humans. It may not even be appropriate to apply the term selfishness to animals."

"But you include the selfish gene as part of the process of evolution," Prosecutor interjected. "From what you said earlier, I was under the impression that arrogance and selfishness were negative emotions to embrace."

"Ah, the degree of selfishness and arrogance that one acquires is the fundamental ingredient leading him down the evolutionary path of life. Some degree of selfishness is required to survive. A completely altruistic person couldn't live. For example, a man walking down a street stumbles across a homeless person. He observes the homeless person having no money, living day-to-day begging for spare change. A completely selfless person would give the homeless person his house, car, bank account, and job. By doing so, the selfless person is leaving himself in the same position that the homeless person was in. It wouldn't make any sense, as it would put his own survival in jeopardy. Instead, he could do other things to help. For instance, he could lobby the government for increased funding to programs dedicated to ending homelessness. He could also make a financial contribution to an anti-poverty organization, or volunteer at a soup kitchen."

"He's maintaining his own existence and future stability," Prosecutor said, "but also doing his part to help end homelessness. He is exhibiting a degree of selfishness, but it is not destructive selfishness."

"Exactly. He has to consider his own future. I don't believe that is excessive selfishness, since it is only practical and logical. Those who cast homeless people aside, viewing them as inferior or not worth helping, have committed themselves totally to the selfish gene."

"Aha!" Prosecutor shouted. "You are saying the selfish gene is one that can be adopted either as a whole or to a lesser degree. It is Man's adoption of this gene that determines his path of evolution.

"Yes," Noah said, "and it is Man who consciously chooses how he is going utilize this gene, whether for good, bad or evil. The selfish gene cannot be considered evil, because it is how Man adopts and implements this gene in his daily life that is the underlying factor determining his future."

"Will you give me an example?"

Noah reflected for a few seconds as Prosecutor leaned back in his chair and closed his eyes.

"Yes, you see, just because the Holocaust happened doesn't mean that there was no other way. World powers chose to look the other way, their silence condoning the Nazi's behavior. Had the allies chosen to fight earlier, it is certainly possible that millions of lives could have been saved. It could be argued that the world is responsible for the Holocaust.

"Also, the investigation of the holocaust that took place in Rwanda in 1994 has shown that the United Nations were told the slaughter would happen, but they did nothing to prevent it."

"Okay," Prosecutor said. "From what you have argued so far, I believe I can interpret your argument: When a child enters the world, he is basically a helpless lump of clay. His survival depends on the actions of his parents. As the child grows, learning becomes an essential requirement for survival. How he interprets the world depends on his parents and his social environment.

"When born, a primitive form of the selfish gene is part of his makeup. How the selfish gene evolves depends on the child's teachers, that is, his parents and society. In essence, external elements play a major role in the child's future moral code.

"So, if the child is raised with the belief that hatred and superiority are natural emotions to feel, there is a good chance the child will adopt these beliefs and incorporate them into his perception of morality."

"Exactly," Noah said. "When a child enters the world, he starts his life free of hate and evil. It is how he is taught, and what he is taught, that become the ingredients shaping his moral character.

"In essence, humans are born good, but acquire their ethics and morals through learning. So the adults who pass on their beliefs, whether good or bad, basically have the power to either eliminate immorality from the evolutionary ladder, or perpetuate it."

Prosecutor stared at the illustrations on the blackboard and frowned.

"There is something I'm not clear about," he said. "You have divided Have society into two groups: the Haves and the Have-Less. Are you saying that there aren't any Have-Nots?"

"There are Have-Nots," Noah replied, "but I wouldn't define them as Have-Nots. They are more like casualties of a gluttonous quest to control the process of evolution. They are living proof of the new amorality adopted by the Haves, and their presence reveals how, in a world approaching six billion humans, it is morally wrong to allow a handful of Phibs to take control of everything."

"So," Prosecutor said in a frosty voice, "if adults are responsible for the continual evolutionary passage of the self-deception gene, I don't see any hope for humanity."

"Now we are at a critical point in evolution. If you look carefully at my chart, you will see that within the excessive selfishness, self-deception and evil, the essence of humanity is revealed. What I propose to do now is to eliminate the dark passages. By doing so, I will reveal my fundamental evidence."

Noah proceeded to the blackboard and erased everything. He turned toward Prosecutor, and this time, it was he who revealed the mischievous smile.

"Are you ready?"

Prosecutor laughed and said, "I'm as ready as I will ever be."

The Sinking of Noah's Ark

The Story of the Aphibs

→ *Aphibs I*

<u>*Selfish Gene*</u> → *Truth* → *Self Realization Gene* → *Higher Consciousness*

Lie   *Creator*

Conditional Acceptance   *True Morality*

→ *Aphibs II*
→ *Moral Creator* → *Unknowing Atheism* → *Morality*

Noah returned to his seat while Prosecutor and the Jury studied the chart. They grinned. Noah hoped that they admired his work and chose to resume before the smiles turned into scowls.

"As I said earlier, there is a wide scope of people refusing to embrace the Lie, and there are those who embrace it, but not in its entirety. I am arguing that it is these individuals that are the reason why the Creator shouldn't eliminate the human race; for if the human race is eliminated, goodness and innocence will also be wiped out. The Creator, the embodiment of goodness, cannot execute such a task because it is a violation of everything he stands for. Therefore, as long as goodness exists, then evolution, must as you say, continue on its merry way, even if it means the evil gene still flourishes."

Noah looked at Prosecutor; his eyes were closed. After a moment, he opened them and looked directly into Noah's eyes. Noah searched for defeat but saw, for the first time, recognition. He was not exactly sure how to interpret the expression.

"I have to confess," Prosecutor said, "you are almost there."

Almost there? Noah thought. *What more is there to say?*

"I cannot allow the verdict to be read until one further matter has been addressed. This would be the future of your species, as well as the other species residing on your world."

"I don't know if I can be of much help. I'm afraid that I cannot see into the future."

Prosecutor laughed and said, "No, I don't want to know exactly what will happen. I want to know if it *can* happen."

Noah reflected for a moment.

"Oh, I understand. You want to know if the truth will prevail? If it is indeed possible?"

"Yes," Prosecutor said, "your track record leaves much to be desired."

"That's true, but I believe the possibility still exists in spite of our notorious past."

"Well, let's hear it."

Noah shifted awkwardly in his seat.

"In order to prove that the possibility still exists, I have to shed light on where we are now, although it will initially make my case appear weak."

"That's okay," Prosecutor chuckled. "Your testimony won't be entered into the record until you have finished speaking."

Noah cleared his throat. "Today, the Phibs have become a society of self-preservationists. They spend so much time hating and blaming each other for the problems of the world, that at the end of the day, they escape the drudgery of their lives by acquiring mounds of useless products. The Phibs have come to live for the day, and not worry about tomorrow. They believe that everything they see on the television and read in the papers is the absolute truth, and are too tired to question. Phib's great dream in life: the lottery numbers finally rolling in so he can leave his mindless, unrewarding job, and live a life of vain happiness."

"Why is Phib society so obsessed with material goods?"

"It's a quick fix to the problems of the real world," Noah replied. "It gives a false sense of happiness. Phib takes and takes, whether he needs it or not, and when he grows bored of it, there is something more improved to briefly entertain him. Basically, Phibs have become lazy and stopped caring. They have become morally impaired."

"But," Prosecutor interrupted, "there are those still embracing the evil gene."

"Yes, I agree the evil gene is still around, but the difference is that now society has evolved to a higher condition, prohibiting those embracing the evil gene from ever having the power Hitler once held. They will never have the power to set up death camps. African-Americans will never be forced out of America or into slavery. The only power the evil gene has is terrorism. So, humans have made some achievements."

"Terrorism is an achievement?"

"No, terrorism is the evil gene's futile attempt to gain control of the process of evolution. But there are many others who denounce evil. You see, throughout human history, there have been individuals who have evolved inwardly to a higher state of consciousness. They are said to have realized the *true nature of the self*. Such people are examples of the limitless possibilities.

"Biologically and genetically speaking, there is nothing unusual about them. They are the same as everyone else, but the only difference is that they have broken free of a self-limiting world filled with useless trinkets, and achieved inner peace. In the past, the number of people who have made this transition has been small, but because of the new technological era we are living in, many more of these individuals are discovering that life itself is not pre-determined, and it is these individuals feared most by the evil gene. They seek peace and evolution to higher moral consciousness, while the latter seek war and de-evolution to deteriorated immoral consciousness."

"If these individuals are scattered all over the world, how can they make a difference?"

"Years ago, no one believed that through all of our differences, there is one common thread linking us all, Mother Earth—the planet that gave us life.

"Amidst all of our differences, Mother Earth is the root we all share. The world itself has become united with one major problem seeking to affect us all. Our planet is on the verge of dying. There are many crises now dwelling around us, such as global warming, depletion of our natural resources, disappearing rainforests, polluted rivers, desertification, famine and disease, and a growing gap between the rich and the poor. As each day goes by, more and more people are beginning to realize that, God or no God, we are the only ones who can fix it.

"It is becoming clear that as the global economy becomes more centralized, there are a handful of Haves at the helm of this globalization boat not looking to the future. Their power is corrupting them, and they have a greedy desire to hold on to the power at any cost. This small group of individuals have single-handedly taken over the evolutionary process, and if permitted, will eventually allow the process to end."

"Are you saying the planet is dying as a result of human greed?"

"Yes, most definitely. As I said, the planet that once provided us with an abundance of riches is now being destroyed. Sadly, the deaths currently resulting from the deterioration of the planet are being seen in the Have-Not world, because they lack the materials needed to sustain them. The Haves are accumulating it all, and are reluctant to share, but the illness is slowly making its way to the Have world. We see this with excessive flooding, depletion of our fish stocks, hurricanes and tornadoes, and oil wells and reserves that are slowly dwindling away."

"And God isn't responsible?" Prosecutor asked.

"No. What is happening to our planet is of our own making, and we are responsible for the suffering taking place. It would be arrogant of one to blame God for not stepping in to clean up the mess. It's becoming clear that we are going to fix it, or die as a result of our ignorance."

"The mess that you mention, why do you think it has taken place?"

"What has happened," Noah said, "is that after all of the horrible events that have taken place in human history, God has not made his physical presence known to the world, and those in power assume that no such being exists. With no one to answer to, greed becomes a much more desirable emotion to embrace."

"If the elite feel they have no one to answer to, how do they justify their actions to the masses?"

"That is simple to illustrate," Noah replied. "For instance, evolutionary psychologists justify current choices and actions by comparing modern Man to early Man. Some of the current comparisons are frivolous. For example, they like to provide trivial information explaining why women tend to gravitate toward *chick flicks*, and men to *dick flicks*.

Prosecutor and the Jury snickered.

"But there are other comparisons being made that I feel are more dangerous," Noah continued. "For example, individuals are taught to rely solely on instinct, not emotions, when making decisions. We see this clearly in the corporate world. Evolutionary psychologists twist the actions of early Man to fit in with current situations. They compare the Stone Age people's alliances to that of big corporations.

"So, when a company chooses to maximize profits and eliminate the competition, Man is said to be acting as his tribal ancestors did. Therefore, evolutionary psychology would tell us that clear-cutting forests, and dumping toxic wastes into our oceans and streams are just examples of Man acting according to his genetic design, his destiny."

"What does this all signify?"

"It signifies that Man is now absolved from all unethical activities. Evolutionary psychology is telling us that we are what we are, and cannot change, so we may as well accept our fate. It terrifies me to know there are some psychologists out there claiming violent acts such as road rage are the result of a genetic predisposition to excessive violence, that Man is inherently prone to feeble-minded acts of violence.

"Basically, this new *technological/scientific amorality* is seeking to claim us all, and I don't believe this new morality is acceptable."

"Why?"

"Because then you would have to believe that the Jewish Holocaust, the native peoples' destruction, and African slavery are natural occurrences. Evolutionary psychology takes the most vicious emotions and actions of pre-modern Man era, and modifies them to justify Man's thoughts, behavior, and actions today. Evolutionary psychology solely emphasizes the biological and genetic origin of moral values, and ignores the capability of learning to shape morality."

"So," Prosecutor interrupted, "there is a strong trend to condone Man's past, present and future. The whole basis of discovering how Man came to be is driven by self-preservation. For example, it ensures the Haves maintain control by keeping guilt out of the boardroom. The Haves can't question their choices and actions, because if they do, their ivory towers, like Newton's apple, will come tumbling down."

"Yes. Debunking morality and free will is the fundamental goal of technological amorality."

"So how in Hell do you expect to solve this problem?" Prosecutor asked. "From what you have told me so far about human evolution, it seems an impossible task."

"Not an impossible task, just a difficult one. You see, the problem does lie in our genetic makeup. Our path has not been one of cooperation."

"How does one get a world of prejudice and hate to cooperate?"

"Well," Noah said, "by exposing the Lie. The fundamental question the human race must ask itself is: If this truth that I have been taught to believe in is actually a lie, then what is it I am being lied to about, and why? What are the Haves afraid will happen if I discover the truth behind the Lie?

"Those who have always felt powerless to make change are mobilizing themselves to save humanity, and the other species. Unfortunately, these small groups of individuals have yet to gain the needed power. The problem is that people have attached themselves to one particular cause, and dedicated themselves to that cause."

"What's wrong with doing that?"

"Absolutely nothing, but looking at in a global perspective, it makes positive change too slow in comparison to our ailing planet. So what we now have are thousands of different groups fighting for thousands of important causes, but they fail to realize that the economic elites are merging into one united force. Can you imagine what the world would be like if all of the different groups did the same? It would be incredible."

"Why do you think this has not happened?"

"To do this," Noah said, " the individuals in each of the groups will have to find a way to let go of their past prejudices and superiority complexes, and abandon everything they have been taught. One lesson history has taught us is: No matter how many times we are piled together into one psychological analysis, we are in fact not the same. We are easy to manipulate, but we are just as easily prone to individual thinking that goes against the norm."

"Basically," Prosecutor said, "each individual has to wipe the evolutionary slate clean and start rebuilding a new foundation of morals and ethics, a foundation void of hate, prejudice, and excessive selfishness."

"Yes. They must revamp their entire genetic makeup on an individual level. The key to achieving such an immense task is realizing that we aren't at the mercy of mind-controlling genes. As long as we continue to remain separate from each other, change will not occur fast enough to stop the death of the planet. This can't happen by simply changing our behavior. For instance, a person doesn't become a non-racist simply by shocking him every time he makes a racial slur."

"So," Prosecutor interrupted, "once Man discovers his true self, can he then modify his behavior to adapt to the changes that must be made? Decoding the Lie is imperative for the future of your species."

"Yes: ageism, sexism, racism, homophobia, speciesism, and classism are all linked by one common strand. There is a strong desire to oppress, hate and control out there. It may differ from one group to another, but underneath the motives are the same."

"How do the "isms" stay alive? I mean, how are they passed down from one generation to the next?"

"There are many ways this is done, but there is one major way the "isms" are kept alive. Parents and society continue their passage by killing a crucial element of a child's development—imagination."

"How do they kill imagination?"

"Many methods have been employed, but there is one efficient way Phibs kill imagination. Some parents prevent their children from reading books that encourage the exercise of imagination and creativity. For instance, they may not allow them to read books about magical worlds and sorcerers. They believe such stories encourage children to practice witchcraft."

Prosecutor rolled his eyes.

"Once they have successfully killed their child's imagination," Noah continued, "they can then mold the child in an image of themselves."

"What are the implications of killing a child's imagination?"

"It means gun manufacturers and psychiatrists will never be out of business."

"Okay," Prosecutor sighed, "what do you think your survival depends on?"

"Exposing and decoding the original Lie. We have come to believe that those in power know what is best for us, and if we do nothing and allow a small group of individuals shape the future, than we will suffer the consequences. This manufactured reality is not our only reality. Once we rid ourselves of the fear of change, we will be in a better state to cope."

"After decoding the lies, and the original Lie is revealed, what will it mean?"

"We will discover why the original Lie was created in the first place, and when we discover that answer, we will discover the truth behind the Lie."

"What will that reveal?"

"It will reveal the source of the Light. You see, our task is to manifest this change and incorporate it into a new way of living. We must ask ourselves: Are the planet and the human consciousness one entity? If our conscious thoughts deteriorate, will the planet deteriorate?"

"Unfortunately," Prosecutor intervened, "there is still an extensive group of individuals who have yet to realize the crisis of the situation."

"Yes, it seems that if there is nothing apparently wrong with our immediate surroundings, then there must be nothing wrong elsewhere. As long as our grocery counters remain stocked, then we assume everything is fine. I believe this is deteriorating thought, and it's this pattern of thinking that has led to the current state of the planet."

"Aha!" Prosecutor bellowed. "You are saying that if the self-realization gene is proven to exist, it will be readily embraced."

"Yes, but it won't be readily accepted by everyone. The self-realization gene has always existed. The self-deception gene has often overpowered or masked it, but it has never been destroyed. We see this today in the fight to save our planet, the fight to end poverty, racism, oppression, human exploitation, and the animal holocaust. In spite of the evil that has flourished throughout history, you cannot disregard those who have fought and triumphed against it."

"And you feel that the changes are possible?"

"I don't know for sure if we can achieve this," Noah said, "but I believe wiping humans off the face of the earth would be an illogical act, because you would be wiping out human virtue as well. As long as there are self-realized individuals that walk the earth, then I suppose there is...hope.

"Once human beings acquired free will, intellect, and a sense of morality, the future fell out of the Creator's hands. Whatever the outcome, we are solely accountable."

"What do you think the outcome will be?"

"I have no idea what the eventual outcome will be, but I believe through our choices or lack thereof, there are two possible, although, they are only my truth."

"That's okay," Prosecutor laughed. "This is what the trial has been all about."

Noah proceeded to the blackboard and picked up the chalk, feeling nauseated. He knew this illustration would be critical to his defense.

Without looking at Prosecutor, he said, "I will now chart out two possible outcomes that will be of our own making:

EVOLUTION OF THE HUMAN PSYCHE
The Phibs Future

*Truth →Free Will →Seeing ****** Denying*

Evil Gene Flourishes

Hate

*Touching ********* Destroying*

Deterioration of planet   Oppression/War
Survival of the fittest   Poverty and Famine

*Hearing **************** Silencing*

*Accept the individual is powerless *The ones in power remain selfish and greedy *Not worrying about the future of our planet *Only the wealthy and powerful adapt *Eventual destruction of our planet *Eventual destruction of planets' resources. Billions die from war, disease and natural disasters

Deteriorated Consciousness

The End

TrysDan Roberts

EVOLUTION OF THE HUMAN PSYCHE
The Aphibs Future

*Free Will →Truth →Seeing*********** Conceiving*

Self-Realization Gene Flourishes

*Hearing *************** Listening*

*Self discovery **Debunking the Superior Complex*
*Empowerment **Releasing prejudice*
* Inner peace **Globalization of Truth*

*Touching **************** Creating*

*Adjusting our lifestyles *Eradicating the Evil Gene in the majority of the population *Peacefully forcing those in power to act responsibly *Recognizing Moral Responsibilities

Higher Consciousness

Creator *Unknowing Atheism*
Discovering the Soul *Discovering the spirit of humanity*

The Beginning

Noah walked to his seat as Prosecutor released a loud, "Hmm."

"What do you mean by recognizing moral responsibilities?"

"We have to realize that suffering is not a truth in life. For example, the suffering in the Have-Not world has become a greedy financial opportunity for the Have world, as they use human compassion to make a fortune. As I said earlier, there are those who selflessly dedicate their lives to fight famine in these countries, spending tireless hours raising funds to bring food to the starving. This food is being provided by Have industry; therefore, the Haves can produce as much food as they want because they know there will be a never-ending demand. As the population increases in the Have-Not world, so do corporate bank accounts in the Have world.

"Instead of assisting the Have-Nots with the tools and technology needed to become self-sufficient, they continue to drop bags upon bags of their products upon them. In essence, through greed, the corporate Haves played a major part in the current situation."

"I suppose it would be immoral to say: *Well, we gave them all this food and the population is still increasing. I guess we had better stop helping.*"

"Yes, it would," Noah replied. "The Have world is equally responsible for the current situation. By making their selfish choices, the Haves have become part of the problem."

"Okay," Prosecutor said, "there is one more statement in your chart that is confusing me. Can you explain your interpretation of the Creator and unknowing atheism?"

"When I say discovering the soul, I mean discovering the true Creator, that is, a higher power of all-goodness, void of prejudice, hate, and superiority. It is a power that we do not make demands from, and sees us all as equals and responsible for our own actions.

"When I describe unknown atheism as discovering the spirit of humanity, I refer to those believing that it was science, not God, that created the universe, and humans did not have to evolve to be a selfish and violent species. It was a choice, not a predisposition to it, and our genes did not make us what we are. We made our genes what they are through our own free will, and it was our selfish thoughts and emotions that have resulted in our current genetic makeup. For example, war is not a necessary tool of survival. War results from a selfish desire to control the world."

"But," Prosecutor interrupted, "your species has come to believe that aggression evolved to be a fundamental part of your genetic makeup."

"That pattern of thinking evolved from generations of flawed evolution. There is no reason why we should accept aggression as natural in any species, including our own. We have to accept that many species, including humans, have evolved with the potential to be aggressive. Whether aggression occurs, depends more on experience and societal influences than it does on genetic evolution."

"How do you explain the excessive violence in your culture?"

"Violence can be viewed as learned behavior, becoming an accepted part of the society culture. We chose to embrace it and instill it in our genetic makeup. Everything around us reflects that choice. For example, there are many who blame the media and the entertainment industry for the increase in violence, but I disagree. The images we see on television and in the movies are merely a reflection of ourselves. We are obsessed with violence, so much so that we have become desensitized to it."

"The electronic media is nothing more than a business," Prosecutor interrupted. "In order to make a profit, the television and film industry have to satisfy customer needs. It is the same old story of blaming someone else for the problems of the world."

"Exactly. If the masses did not want violence on television, the entertainment industry wouldn't provide it."

"But," Prosecutor said, "you said earlier that there are scientists and researchers who compare animal aggression to human aggression."

"We have to be careful about comparing animal aggression to human warfare. Animals may fight to win a territory, a mate, or obtain food, but this is much different from a soldier dropping an atomic bomb on thousands of people, instantly incinerating them alive without ever looking into their eyes. By recognizing the difference, we will have the ability to make the world better. We have to look inwardly and ask ourselves: Is this reality that I live in the only reality possible?

"There is still time to reach a higher state of consciousness, whether that is by discovering the true Creator, or becoming an unknowing atheist. Either way you look at it, there really is not much difference, as the results will be the same."

"But, there are those who say achieving that kind of enlightenment is impossible."

"I would say to them: Look at the survivors of the atrocities in human history, look at what emerged from the ruins—life. Also, look at all of the people fighting for causes now. The possibility is still there, and will remain there until the last human takes his final breath.

"Because the foundation of our existence is in danger of being destroyed, enlightenment has become more crucial than ever. As I said earlier, this foundation—Mother Earth."

In the midst of Noah's testimony the white Light suddenly emerged. Prosecutor rose from his seat and walked toward him. Noah realized that he had better make his conclusion quickly.

"Whatever happens will happen because of our actions, and if we do nothing and continue to live in a morally impaired state, then the future will reflect our choice. In the end, how we got here will be not important. Why we got here will be the ultimate question."

By the time Noah finished his sentence, the Light had completely surrounded him. The white hiding under the gray of the walls pushed its way through. Prosecutor was standing, wearing the most beautiful smile Noah had ever seen, his eyes a glorious, penetrating white light. It gripped Noah's being.

"Wait," Noah shouted, "this light feels different. It's not the same as before."

Prosecutor said nothing, his smile sedating Noah.

"I won't be going back to Aidan, will I?" he croaked.

"No," Prosecutor whispered gently, "you will not."

At this point, the light was so blinding Noah could hardly see Prosecutor. He realized suddenly that the verdict had already been brought down. He looked in bewilderment at Prosecutor and the Jury. The Jury stood, turned away from Noah, and vanished into the light.

"Wait," Noah calls out, "what is the verdict? Is God guilty?"

Prosecutor laughed and said, "What verdict, Noah? I thought by now you would have realized who was actually on trial."

Prosecutor and the Light had merged into one blazing entity. Noah was overcome with a new emotion—peace.

"You're not the Prosecutor or the Devil," Noah cried. "Oh damn, you are..."

"Noah," he said, "I am what you want me to be. It has always been that way. You know this. Take it with you."

On those final words, tears began to stream down Noah's cheeks. He closed his eyes and willingly surrendered to the Light.

The Sinking of Noah's Ark

Chapter IX

As Noah struggled to open his eyes, light pierced them. There was no longer any warmth accompanying it. He discovered its source was a penlight. A man was hovering eagerly over him, shining the burning light into his eyes. Noah strained to raise his hand, pushing the light away. The man stepped back, revealing green surgical scrubs and a stained white lab coat. Noah gazed wearily at him. He was a young man, probably fresh out of medical school.

"Noah, can you hear me? Do you know where you are?" he asked anxiously.

Noah spied his mother standing a few feet away from the doctor with a worried look in her eyes.

"Yes, I can hear you," he choked.

"You received a serious blow to your head," the doctor said, "but it looks like you will make it. We just have to run a few tests to make sure you did not suffer any internal head injuries."

Head injuries? Noah felt more like someone had driven an ice pick through his head.

Marta approached her son, her eyes showing more lines than he remembered. Slipping her hand in his, she gave him a gentle squeeze.

"I am okay now, Mom."

Marta's eyes filled with tears.

A gruff voice next to them broke the silence. "Looks like God was watching over you, young fella."

Glancing over at the bed next to him, he saw a frail old man hooked up to an array of machines.

He smiled. "Yes sir, seatbelts are a marvelous creation."

Following the discharge from the hospital, Marta and her son began the journey home. During the trip, Noah recounted the events, and as he told the story, Marta drove steadily, nodding her head and smiling. It was as if what he was saying was a normal, everyday occurrence. Noah figured that she believed he really did experience it, and neglected to suggest the events may have been a result of the head trauma. He realized that it really didn't matter, since he couldn't prove or disprove its truthfulness. All he could do was tell the story.

After he finished, Marta made only one comment. She said that the hospital that Noah had recovered in was the same hospital he had been born in.

Noah never returned to the university. Along with the blow to the head, he had suffered a broken leg and arm, making his semester a total write-off. He had his belongings packed up and sent home by bus. Upon receiving them, he was surprised to see how his life could be put in such small boxes. Now that his father was gone, he had decided it would be best to stay and help his mother make the transition to widowhood. It was a difficult passage for her. For such a long time, her life was interwoven with Paul's. They had functioned as one being. His death was as though her arm had been cut off, and she now had to adjust to life without it. She managed to do so; she had an amazing inner strength.

Noah spent the next three years obtaining his teacher's degree through correspondence classes from the university. During the period it took to complete his degree, he spent much of his free time exploring the community and its inhabitants. Although he was familiar with the streets, buildings and residents, it felt like they were all strangers. He was looking at them through different eyes, and what he saw when he gazed around could only be described in one word—home.

The houses and people were brighter than he remembered. As each year went by, the population slowly dwindled. Even so, Noah never felt lonely. He even took the time to talk to Mr. Weatherfield, and for the first time in his life he knew exactly how he fit into this world and accepted it unconditionally.

The completion of Noah's education degree was accompanied by a stroke of good timing. A teacher at his old high school was retiring, and he was offered the position. He readily accepted.

Now, when he stands in the front of the classroom and stares into the unknowing eyes of his students, he realizes that the information he passes on to them will play a big part in shaping their future. So what does Noah pass on to his protégés? I suppose the only thing he has to offer them—choice. How does he pass on choice? By revealing the fork in the road lying before them. Once they embark on their journeys, all Noah can do is pray that they don't choose the most seductive path.

My son, Noah, completed the circle that he drew for himself so long ago. It was an old fisherman's tale worth sharing. Now, I watch over my beautiful wife and patiently await her arrival. Aidan watches over Noah, and some day we will all embrace in one powerful flame. Until then, I take comfort in knowing that my family has found life again.

It has been almost twelve years since I stepped on the bus and boldly crossed the causeway. Now, when I look at the community, I realize that so much has changed—so much is gone. Most of the old fishing shacks have crumbled. There are now only about a dozen fishing boats remaining. The town is much smaller, as many have left in search of work.

In spite of the decline, the community has somehow survived. Once relying on each other, the residents now depend on outsiders. Every summer, tourists flock to Walden's Cove to capture a glimpse of a historic relic. The dollars dropped into the cash registers of the stores, restaurants, and Bed and Breakfasts sustain us.

Many of the older fishermen converted their vessels into tour boats in an effort to retire with dignity. My father would have been one of those men if nature had not intervened.

The only link to my father's past is this old dory I now inhabit. Every Sunday morning, after dropping my mother off at church, I come down to the once-cluttered wharf, and row out a safe distance from shore. It is during this time, while my mother is reflecting on her own spirituality, that I reflect on mine. Sitting on the water allows me to lose all perception of time. The water that gently laps my boat becomes time waves; the dory, my lifeline. The anger and pain that once ruled my being has dissipated. All I feel now is possibilities.

As the crowds begin to disperse from the church, I see my mother making her way down the hill. Her eyes shine in spite of the lines that have fastened themselves on her face. Her hair is a shiny gray now; even so, she is still beautiful. She projects a powerful strength, a strength neither money nor status can buy.

I start to row to shore—to my present—to my future, leaving the past until next Sunday.

I have yet to produce a child, so I have been forced to break with the family tradition of naming the boat after one's firstborn.

After a few days of considering the possibilities, I finally decide to name her Noah's Ark II.

Hey, what can I say? I am only human. That is the truth.

Well...my truth.

The Sinking of Noah's Ark

Stories Inspiring Noah's Story

Direct quotes are cited from the following sources:

1. Hawking, Stephen. A Brief History of Time.1988
2. De Las Casas, Bartolome. The devastation of the Indians: a brief account
3. Dawkins, Richard. The Selfish Gene,1976
4. Campbell, Neil A. Biology. (3rd ed.), 1987
5. Human evolution: history of man.
   http://www.onelife.com/evolve/manev.html
6. Religion and government.
   http://www.theworldreligion.org/newpage2.htm
7. Primitive religion. http://www.mb-soft.com/believe/txo/primitiv.html
8. Russell, Peter. The evolution of consciousness.
   http://www.peterrussell.com/SCG/EoC.html
9. Atrocities of the Christian church. The art of medieval torture.
   http://cgibin.erols.com/bdwilner/.../history/
10. The biological basis of morality: Part 1 and 2.
    http://www.theatlantic.com/issues/98apr/bio2.htm
11. The Holocaust: a tragic legacy.
    a) Why could the Holocaust happen?
       http://library.advanced.org/12663/summary/why.html
    b) Genocide.
       http://library.advanced.org/12663/summary/genocide.html
12. The Jewish student on-line research center.
    http://www.us-israel.org/jsource/Holocaust/resist.html
13. Black resistance...slavery in the US.
    a) Africa to America.
       http://www.afroam.org/history/slavery/africa.html
    b) There were no docile slaves.
       http://www.afroam.org/history/slavery/docile.html
    c) Women resisted.
       http://www.afroam.org/history/slavery/women.html
14. A brief history of the Civil Rights Movement.
    http://www.fred.net/nhhs/project/views/histcivilrights.htm
15. Menton, David. Phd. The religion of nature: Social Darwinism.
    http://www.gennet.org/Metro15.htm
16. The Nizkor Project: OSS psychological profile of Hitler, Part 1,2,3,4,5.
    http://www.nizkor.org/hweb/people/h/hitler_adolf/oss_papers/text/
17. Rogers, Ted W. The revolution will be televised.
    http://www.freedonia.com/ctheory/r-revolution_will_be.html
18. Johnson, Robert L. The Bible's unholy origins.
    http://www.deism.com/biblevotes.htm
19. Article 12 of 12. Darwin's minds. (Charles Darwin) (Evolution of

Human Behavior, Part I) (cover story) Bruce Bower. Science news, Oct 12, 1991, v.140,n 15,p. 232(3)
20. Nicholson, Nigel. How hard-wired is human behavior? (Evolution Psychology) Harvard Business Review, July-August 1998. V.76, n.4, p. 134(14)
21. Aquinas, Thomas. The First-Cause Argument

Bible References:

1. Exodus 21:1-6
   God gives guidelines for the selling, buying and treatment of slaves.
2. Numbers 25:9
   24,000 people die in a plague from the Lord.
3. Psalms 19: 5-6
   The sun moves around the earth.
4. Jeremiah 31:37
   This verse implies that the earth does not move
5. Ezekial 7:2
   To Ezekial, the earth is flat and has four corners
6. Matthew 9:32, 12:22, 17: 14-18 and Luke 11:14, 9:39-42
   Epilepsy, blindness, and the inability to speak are caused by demonic possession
7. Ezekial 9:4-6
   The Lord said, "...slay old men outright, young men and maidens, little children and women..."
8. Genesis 7:20-23
   God caused a worldwide flood, killing innocent men, women, children and animals. This made him the largest mass murderer in history.

Printed in the United States
6053